SUMMERTIME ISLAND

Books by Erskine Caldwell

ALL NIGHT LONG, 1942 • ALL-OUT ON THE ROAD TO SMO-LENSK, 1942 • AMERICAN EARTH, 1930 • AROUND ABOUT AMERICA, 1964 • THE BASTARD, 1929 • CALL IT EXPERI-ENCE, 1951 • CERTAIN WOMEN, 1957 • CLAUDELLE INGLISH, 1958 • CLOSE TO HOME, 1962 • THE COURTING OF SUSIE BROWN, 1952 • DEEP SOUTH, 1968 • EPISODE IN PALMETTO, 1950 • GEORGIA BOY, 1943 • GOD'S LITTLE ACRE, 1933 • GRETTA, 1955 • GULF COAST STORIES, 1956 • A HOUSE IN THE UPLANDS, 1946 • IN SEARCH OF BISCO, 1965 • JENNY BY NATURE, 1961 • JOURNEYMAN, 1935 • KNEEL TO THE RISING SUN, 1935 • A LAMP FOR NIGHTFALL, 1952 • THE LAST NIGHT OF SUMMER, 1963 • LOVE AND MONEY, 1954 • MISS MAMMA AIMEE, 1967 • MOS-COW UNDER FIRE, 1942 • PLACE CALLED ESTHERVILLE, 1949 • POOR FOOL, 1929 • SOME AMERICAN PEOPLE, 1935 • SOUTH-WAYS, 1938 • THE SURE HAND OF GOD, 1947 • THIS VERY EARTH, 1948 • TOBACCO ROAD, 1932 • TRAGIC GROUND, 1944 • TROUBLE IN JULY, 1940 • WE ARE THE LIVING, 1933 • WHEN YOU THINK OF ME, 1959 • WRITING IN AMERICA, 1967

For Children

MOLLY COTTONTAIL, 1958 • THE DEER AT OUR HOUSE, 1966

Anthologies of Erskine Caldwell

THE COMPLETE STORIES OF ERSKINE CALDWELL, 1953 • THE HUMOROUS SIDE, EDITED BY ROBERT CANTWELL, 1951 • STORIES, EDITED BY HENRY SEIDEL CANBY, 1944

By Erskine Caldwell and Margaret Bourke-White

NORTH OF THE DANUBE, 1939 • RUSSIA AT WAR, 1942 • SAY: IS THIS THE U.S.A.?, 1940 • YOU HAVE SEEN THEIR FACES, 1937

SUMMERTIME ISLAND

by

Erskine Caldwell

AN BOOK

THE WORLD PUBLISHING COMPANY
NEW YORK   CLEVELAND

Published by The New American Library, Inc.
in association with
The World Publishing Company
2231 West 110th Street, Cleveland, Ohio

Library of Congress Catalog Card Number: 68-28111

Printed in the United States of America

TO

Lieutenant Andrew Fletcher III

ONE

1

It was the second week of June in Unionville, a town of almost five thousand people in the northwestern corner of Tennessee and not far from Kentucky, where I had gone to spend two months of the summer.

Unionville had an imposing colonnaded gray-stone county courthouse and a small brick jail with iron-barred windows and two red fire trucks with solid-rubber tires but at that time it had very few paved streets and most of the sidewalks were graveled paths. It was a place where most of the lawyers and doctors and wealthy storekeepers in those days lived in large white houses that had been built far apart—often one of them being the only house on an entire block—and nearly all of those had wide lawns and tall oak trees around them.

Except for brief intervals when the *Panama Limited* and other fast Illinois Central passenger trains roared through Unionville with whistles screaming, it was quiet all over town and like being far away in the country after the city noises of Memphis where the week before I had finished the second year of high school. Aunt Rosemary and Uncle Guthry Henderson, who had no children of their own, lived in one of the large white houses on Glenwood Street near the city limits and they kept two young sorrel horses in a nearby pasture that had whitewashed crisscross boarding for the fencing and a three-sided stable for shelter in cold and rainy weather.

My uncle, who was my father's only brother, was a tall, dark-haired, friendly-mannered man in his forties and he owned a hardware and farm supply store on Madison Street just around the corner from the courthouse square. When I got to Unionville on the evening train from Memphis, he had said I could help him unpack freight shipments and stock the shelves and learn something about business that summer. Then he told me that when there was nothing for me to do in the store I could go around town and make friends with boys and girls my own age—I was almost sixteen years old then—and go swimming and ride the horses and do anything else that interested me.

As it happened though, before I got to know anybody of my own age in Unionville or had time to ride the horses, there were several heavy wooden crates to be opened in the rear of the store the first morning I was there. We had unpacked about half of the shipment when my uncle dropped his clawhammer and sat down on one of the crates. After pushing his hair from his forehead, he lighted his cigar again. Then for the next several minutes he did not say a word while he stared thoughtfully at the big stack of kitchenware we had un-crated.

"Look here, Steve," he said presently, suddenly turn-ing his head and staring at me with a slight smile and a nodding of his head. He puffed quickly on the cigar several times. "Tell me something I've been wondering about, Steve. You've never gone off before on a real fishing trip, have you? I mean, a camp-out fishing trip for four or five days on the big river—the Mississippi—for catfish trotlining. You've never done that, have you?"

He looked very pleased and nodded his head faster and puffed on the cigar some more when I told him that I had only fished in creeks and ponds and had never done anything like that. It was as if he had been hoping I would say exactly what I did.

"That's fine!" he said enthusiastically, pounding the top of one of the crates with his fist. "That's great! It's exactly what I was figuring on. There'll be plenty of time during the rest of the summer for you to ride the horses and get to know some young people and things like that. Let's hurry and get the rest of this stuff price-marked and put on the shelves. Right now is the best time of the whole year for river fishing. Did you know that, Steve? You got here at just the right time. If we get everything ready today, we can get up and leave early tomorrow morning. What do you think of that, Steve? There's nothing better to put a man's feet in your shoes for you when you're at your age—a fishing camp-out down there on the river. It'd be a real shame for me not to take you down there right away for your own good. It'll be something you'll remember all your life.

"It's been I don't know how long since the last time I was down there and you make it the best reason in the world to go to the river now. I've felt a fishing fever coming over me the past few warm days, but I didn't know what I could do about it till you got here. Now, don't say anything at all about this to your Aunt Rosemary—I'll do the talking. I'll just tell her that you need to go and that I ought to take you for your own good. That's the best way to handle it. If there's too much talk about it beforehand, she could think up some excuses why I can't take you and we don't want to run that risk and have that happen. Your Aunt Rosemary doesn't think much of men going off by themselves for camp-out fishing and she can get mighty suspicious about it. I don't want her to get out of sorts about this because I want her to be agreeable to keep the store open for me while we're gone. I couldn't afford to close up the store at this time of year for nearly a week and lose all that business."

He reached for the clawhammer and stood up.

"There's one more thing, Steve," he said seriously, looking closely at the claw on the hammer as if he had never inspected one before. "I've come to a conclusion about something else. You're growing up to be a man now and are already as tall as I am. And now that we're going off fishing together, I don't want you to call me Uncle Guthry after this. Starting right now. You're get-

4

ting too grown-up for that. Call me Guthry—that's all. Just Guthry and nothing else. Now, will you remember that, Steve?"

"I think I can—I'll try," I told him.

"That's fine," he said with a wave of his hammer. "That's the way we want it. It's a good way for men to go off fishing together. Everybody first-name and nothing else. But you'd better keep on calling your Aunt Rosemary the same as you've always done—I don't think it'd be suitable any other way."

There were two more crates to open and unpack. While we were busy doing that, Guthry said that as soon as everything was finished he was going off to look for Troy Pickett, who hauled freight and express from the Illinois Central Railroad depot to the stores in town, and get him to go along so we could use one of his trucks to haul everything we needed to camp for four or five days. Not many people owned automobiles and trucks at that time and he said that only somebody like Troy Pickett was enough of a fisherman to take his truck over the kind of dirt road we would have to travel. Besides a sleeping tent and folding cots and some quilts, frying pans and tackle boxes and a lot of other things had to be taken. He said it was twenty miles or more over the rough dirt road from Unionville to a boat landing at a mud flat near a place called Little Dipper where we could rent a fifteen-foot skiff and transfer everything from the truck to the skiff and then row about an eighth of a mile across a backwater slough to Summertime Island.

5

"Don't take my word for it, Steve," he said, smiling happily and hurrying to get the new stock to the bins and shelves. His cigar had gone out but he did not take the time to relight it then. "Just wait till we get there. You'll see good and plenty—it's the finest place up and down the whole river for camping and catfishing. That island is about four or five city blocks long and all of a block wide. It gets covered with muddy floodwater in spring during the upriver run-off, but by the end of May it's high and dry again and these early summer thundershowers soon wash off the mud and drift from the willows so their leaves are bright green like right now in early June. All that pure greenery is a beautiful sight to see.

"That's about the only sure thing you can say about the island, though—the spring flooding and the summer greenery. That meandering big river has a habit of changing course during flood stage and maybe cutting itself a brand-new channel—maybe even making a loopy-de-loop off toward Missouri or even back toward Kentucky. That's why nobody's going to say for sure if Summertime Island is in Tennessee, Kentucky, or Missouri. But it's all the same to me as long as I can go there and get all the catfish I can catch and eat and not lose my Tennessee voting rights. I wouldn't want to be forced to change my politics and have to cast my vote for those rascal politicians up in Kentucky or over in Missouri. I have a hard enough time as it is when it comes to deciding which are the least worst of the rascals to vote for right here in Tennessee."

2

It was midmorning when Guthry left the hardware store to look for Troy Pickett and it was past noon when he came back.

By that time, several men had heard on the street that he was making up a fishing party to go to Summertime Island and they had come to the store and were waiting for him when he got there. Guthry told them that Troy Pickett was going to take his smaller truck, since he had to leave his big truck so his brother could deliver freight and express while he was gone, and that there would not be enough space for any more people.

The three men stayed and argued for a while, trying their best to get Guthry to change his mind, and then finally they went away grumbling and talking about how mean and selfish he was not to let his real friends go along.

"Think nothing of how those people talked about me, Steve," Guthry said after the men had stomped out of the store. "They didn't really mean it. They're touched with fishing fever—just like I am—and they hardly knew what they said about me. This warm weather in early summer brings out fishing fever in nearly everybody, but they'll calm down and won't hold it against me too long. I hate to turn down anybody who likes river fishing as much as I do. And I know all about that prickly

7

feeling you get under your skin when you want to go and can't—you itch all over like you've got hives but can't scratch it away. This's one time it can't be helped, though—they'll just have to stay here and itch and scratch.

"The main thing about this fishing trip we're going on is to take you down there on a camp-out for your own good and too many people riding in Troy Pickett's truck might make it break down before we got halfway to the river. Troy wants to take one more with us, any-how—a colored fellow to help out around the camp—and the four of us will be a full load. Troy's gone off now to look for somebody like that. What we want to do is hurry and get everything ready and have it piled up at the back door so we can load up the truck and make an early start the first thing in the morning. When you're getting ready to go off fishing, you don't want to let the sun come up and catch you standing flat-footed."

In a storage room at the rear of the building were several folding canvas cots, a sleeping tent, and a large prong-footed cooking grid as well as other camping supplies that Guthry kept there so they would always be on hand and ready to load for a fishing trip.

After we had piled everything near the back door to be ready to put on the truck the next morning, Guthry went to the grocery store next door to buy some coffee and Boston baked beans. He said that we were going to have all the fish we could eat but that he would never want to go camping at the river without plenty of chicory coffee and baked beans to bring out the best flavor of fried catfish.

When Guthry came back from the grocery store, he had several bags of ground chicory coffee and a whole case of canned baked beans. While we were putting the coffee and beans with the other supplies, he said he was going to make one more trip to the grocery store to get a bucket of lard and a sack of cornmeal. Before he could leave, though, Troy Pickett came stomping in from the street.

Troy was angry and even before he got to the rear of the store he was cursing and swearing in a loud voice. Being short and stocky, he walked in a slue-footed stride that made him sway from side to side as if daring anybody to get in his way. And with his mouth open, he was even more fearsome and menacing in appearance—several of his teeth were missing and some of the others were black and jagged.

While both were about the same age, Troy was neither as large nor as tall as Guthry, and after having handled heavy freight shipments for many years he had developed bulging muscles in his arms, and his shoulders were broad and thick with strength. With his heavy chin jutting from his scowling face, he was like somebody constantly looking for a bare-knuckle fight for no reason at all. As he came closer, he was opening and closing both fists.

"I'm a sonofabitch!" he shouted in his booming voice. "One of these days I'm going to haul off and beat the living hell out of every goddam nigger in town! And they can round up some more of them and bring them

9

to town and I'll beat hell out of them too! The black bastards!"

He walked to the rolled-up sleeping tent and kicked it as hard as he could.

"They can send everywhere all over the whole country for more of the black bastards and I'll beat the goddam hell out of them as fast as they can haul them here!"

"Now, wait a minute, Troy," Guthry said to him calmly. "Just hold on. Don't come in here and start talking like that without saying what the trouble is. What'd you get so mad about? What happened?"

Taking off his droopy straw hat and slamming it on the floor, Troy sat down on one of the wooden crates. With a sweep of his hand, he wiped away some of the beads of sweat mingling with the sparse yellowish hair on his balding head.

"I'm a sonofabitch! I'll tell you—goddam it!" he said angrily with a fish-eyed glare. He paused long enough to puff up his cheeks and blow out his breath with a whooshing sound. "Them black bastards! You know what I done? I went to all the trouble to go down to their part of town and look up three different niggers to talk to. And took up all my time doing it. And not a stinking one of them would say they'd go with me to the river tomorrow when I told them that's what I wanted them to do. Besides not doing what I told them, all of them made up some kind of excuse that was nothing but a greasy big lie all the way."

"What about Sam Goddard? Did you speak to him?" Guthry asked.

"Even Sam Goddard wouldn't go, neither—and I know he likes river fishing as much as anybody else and always before used to drop what he was doing and go every chance he could. Sam's got no steady job—now or never. All he does is do some yardboy trash-cleaning work around town when he can find it and he could drop that and go fishing anytime he feels like it. After he stood there and told me three times straight he wouldn't go with me, I told Sam he's nothing but a kinky-haired black bastard and that I was going to get even with him for sure and make him sorry for acting like he did—but he still wouldn't say he'd go like I told him to."

"What kind of excuse did Sam Goddard make for not going with us?" Guthry asked. "I've known Sam for a long time and he's always made a habit of going fishing more than anybody else I know."

Troy puffed up his cheeks again and blew out his breath with an even louder whooshing sound.

"He said his wife is sick and ailing and he had to stay home to take care of her—but he knew that was a greasy big lie when he opened his mouth and said it. He was trying to cover up something else and thought he was fooling me. But I can always tell when a nigger's lying to me. He and some other niggers got together and figured they could pay me back by never doing nothing I wanted them to. And I know why, too. They claim I treat them mean—and by God I do treat them like niggers ought to be treated.

"They know what to expect. When I deliver some freight to one of their stores in their part of town, I dump it right in the middle of the street and leave it there. And that's what they complain about. But by God you'll never see no white man like me hand-trucking their freight inside their stores for them and asking them where they want me to set it down to please them. It can stay out there in the street and rot and rust for all I care."

3

TROY STOOD UP and slammed the droopy straw hat on his head. Then he walked over to the sleeping tent and kicked it again as hard as he could.

"There won't be no trip to Summertime Island in my truck, Guthry," he stated with an emphatic jerk of his head. "I ain't going."

"Don't say that, Troy," Guthry protested.

"That's right. You heard me. You might as well pick up all that camping stuff and put it back where it came from. I ain't going down there without a nigger to gut my fish for me and do all the other messy things like a nigger is for. That's no way for a white man to go river fishing. I'm too proud to do their kind of work."

"Hold on, Troy," Guthry pleaded. "We'll figure out something. We've got to go—don't call it off now. I promised Steve to take him river fishing. And I can't go back on my word—it's not like me to promise something and then not do it. You know you still want to go—and you've got a truck and I don't have one. I'll take care of this trouble you're talking about. I'll go find somebody to take with us. I know a colored fellow who likes fishing—I can get him to go along. He's been here in the store to buy fishhooks and lines for creek fishing and he told me he wanted to go down to the river the first chance he got."

"How do you know he won't be like the rest of them who wouldn't go when I talked to them?"

"Don't worry about that, Troy. I know how to talk to him. I'll get him to go. You just say you'll be here the first thing in the morning with your truck and we'll load up and make a real good early start. How about that, Troy?"

"Who is this nigger you're talking about?"

"He moved here from Kentucky not long ago."

Troy was shaking his head. "I never did like no nigger who comes down here from up north."

He turned around and started to walk away.

Guthry hastily moved in front of Troy to keep him from leaving.

"Wait, Troy. Kentucky's only fifteen miles from here. That's not enough to make much difference."

"But it's enough to make niggers act stuck-up when they come down here in Tennessee. What's the name of this one you're talking about?"

"Duke Hopkins."

Troy laughed.

"What'd I tell you? Duke! That's a stuck-up name for a nigger if I ever heard one. Duke! What made him quit with that? Why don't he call himself Prince or King if he thinks he's somebody big?"

"I asked him how he came to be called Duke. He explained how it happened and I believe him."

"What'd he say?"

"He said his proper first name is Paducah and he was named that by his parents for the place where he was born in Kentucky and that everybody has always shortened it to Duke. That's reasonable. If you had a name like Paducah, you'd want it to be shortened. Now, wouldn't you, Troy?"

"I reckon so," he agreed after a moment. "Go ahead and tell him he can go along. But I'll tell you this much right now. He won't stay stuck-up long around me. I know how to put any nigger in his place—and keep him there. Tell him to be here on time in the morning to load the truck—and not a minute late, neither."

As Troy walked past me, he reached out and shoved me lightly with a thrust of his arm.

"Keep your eyes and ears open on this fishing trip," he told me. "If you do that, you'll learn more being around Troy Pickett than you ever can out of your schoolbooks."

After Troy had walked out of the store, his stubby body swaying with each step, Guthry said if he knew anybody else in town with a truck to take us fishing he would not have anything to do with Troy Pickett for a single minute. He said he had often heard white people boast about how much they hated Negroes, but that Troy, besides boasting about it, would sometimes speed up his truck and make a Negro who was crossing the street jump out of the way to keep from being run over and killed. That was when Guthry said he had made up his mind to save enough money to be able to buy a truck of his own before another summer fishing season came around.

Several customers came into the store and it was about half an hour before they finished buying what they wanted. It was becoming late in the afternoon then, and Guthry hurried next door to get the lard and cornmeal we needed before the grocery store closed.

When he came back, Guthry said that by the time he found Duke Hopkins and had a talk with him, it would be past the time to close the hardware store for the night. He gave me the store keys, showing me how to lock the doors at six o'clock, and told me to be sure to get home in time for supper at seven o'clock because Aunt Rosemary was very particular about promptness at mealtime. Instead of leaving right away to talk to Duke Hopkins, though, he walked back into the store and, with both hands deep in his pockets, leaned against the counter.

"Steve, there's something I want to tell you," he said with a serious frowning, looking straight ahead at the hardware stock on the shelving. He was silent for several moments after that as if thinking about the best way to state what he wanted to say. "We're going down to the river tomorrow on that camp-out fishing trip for several days. And that's a fine thing for you at your age—I mean being down there with men where it's nothing like home—but I think you've had a chance to start learning something right here today. I'm thinking about what Troy said a little while ago—saying you could learn more being around him than you can learn from schoolbooks. Sure, you'll learn something. You'll learn not to admire ignorance and prejudice."

He turned, smiling slightly, and looked at me thoughtfully for a moment.

"Steve," he said then, "I don't mean merely the rough talk of somebody like Troy Pickett. You hear profanity and obscenity wherever you go—it's something you can listen to in Memphis or anywhere else. I'm talking about something entirely different. It's the way Troy talks about colored people—his attitude toward them as people. He really hates them and says so every chance he gets. Not only that, he'll go out of his way to try to hurt them—even kill them. By this time you've already found out that that's the way some people talk and act just as it's the way some people don't. What I'm trying to say now is that there are reasons for the way Troy Pickett talks and acts—and the principal reason is the ignorance of the man. That's what I want to tell you about.

"Troy is like a lot of people. You see them on the street every day. He went to school here in Unionville for only a few years and he barely learned to read and write before he quit going. For several years after that, he was always with a gang of boys that made trouble for Negroes—throwing rocks at them and setting fire to their houses. Later, some killings took place in the country, too.

"Anyway, I was more fortunate. I was able to graduate from high school. That doesn't make me think I'm better than Troy, but I know I'm more sympathetic and tolerant in regard to Negroes than he is. And so after he quit going to school, he grew up and associated with people just as uneducated and ignorant as he was, and that's when their prejudice and cruelty got its start. Now they are the people who use white skin as a threat, like a policeman's billy club, to keep black-skin people down on their knees begging for their lives. That's Troy Pickett—and a lot of other white men. Their breed will have to die out someday, but in the meantime they can do a lot of harm."

Guthry left the counter and went to the door.

"Well, Steve," he called to me without looking backward, "you didn't ask me to preach a sermon, but this was a good time to say what I had on my mind about Troy Pickett. Learning how to hook a catfish won't be the only thing of educational value on this trip down to the river and back. Where else would you be able to study an assortment of people like Troy and Duke and me?"

Walking away then, he went down Madison Street toward the Negro section of town to look for Duke Hopkins.

TWO

1

It was still as dark as the middle of the night and it seemed as if I had been asleep for only a few minutes when Guthry shook me awake and told me to hurry and get dressed to eat breakfast. It was chilly in the house with the damp night air coming through the open windows and it felt more like midwinter than early summer. Shivering in the cold room, I pulled up the covers and tried to wrap them around me.

Guthry turned on all the lights in the room, and, after making sure that I was wide awake and would get out of bed, he walked down the uncarpeted oak-floored hall in his heavy brogan fishing shoes with a jarring rumble that shook the house and would have kept anybody from going back to sleep. When I threw back the covers, the only way to keep from shivering was to get dressed just as fast as I could.

After that, it took me only a few minutes to get to

the kitchen. Aunt Rosemary was there and she had already fried the eggs and ham and cooked grits and made the coffee and the heat of the cookstove had made the whole room comfortably warm.

Guthry was sitting at the kitchen table pouring sorghum molasses on warmed-over biscuits and Aunt Rosemary was standing behind his chair. Now and then she would lean over him and pat one of his cheeks with a light touch of her hand. While he continued eating, she was saying she wanted him to be very careful every minute down on the island. She told him not to shake dice with strangers and to watch out for snakes and to stay away from deep water and not let anything dreadful happen to us. Finally, with a real hard slap on his face, she told him that she had a secret way of knowing if any girls happened to be on Summertime Island while we were there.

Instead of being cross and peevish about our going away on the camping trip, as Guthry had feared the day before, Aunt Rosemary was smiling and pleasant just as if we were only going downtown to open the store for the day's business.

Not only being pretty and girlishly slender, and not nearly as old as Guthry, Aunt Rosemary looked younger than ever that morning with her light brown hair neatly combed and bound over her head with a bright yellow ribbon. She was wearing a thin summer bathrobe over her pale pink nightgown and both of the garments had been made in such a way that her round prominent breasts were only partly covered most of the time. Now and then, when she leaned forward or moved to one side, one of her breasts would burst completely into the open. Each time that happened, she would smile and then carefully cover herself again.

Even though it was stylish at that time for women's clothes to be long, and sometimes almost ankle-length, Aunt Rosemary's scanty bathrobe had been made so that it reached only as far as her knees and had no buttons or other fastenings to keep it closed. And then, too, her nightgown was so short and thin that it was almost as if she were wearing nothing at all under the bathrobe.

"I'm glad girls don't like to go off camping and fishing by themselves for four or five days on an island with no men in sight," she said, leaning over Guthry and hugging him in her arms.

She kissed both sides of Guthry's face and then looked across the table at me.

"How can you stand it, Steve? What will you do without a sweetheart all that time? I bet you already miss your sweetheart in Memphis."

Guthry, sitting up erectly, moved his head until he could see her face.

"Rosemary, how do you know he has a sweetheart in Memphis? A boy his age—"

"Guthry," she said with a chiding inflection of her voice and tightening her arms around him, "Guthry, you know everybody at Steve's age just has to have a sweetheart—or you'd go completely wild and woolly without a girl of some kind. Don't you remember when you were fifteen or sixteen? Or did it happen sooner than that?"

She looked at me again. "Now, tell the truth, Steve. You have a sweetheart in Memphis, don't you?"

When I told her that I knew several girls in Memphis but was not particularly interested in any of them, Aunt Rosemary came around the corner of the table and stood with her hip pressing against my elbow and a hand on my shoulder. An instant later she suddenly stooped over, tightening her arm around my neck, and bit my ear so painfully that I yelled out and tried to push her away at the same time. As soon as my hand touched her breasts, she stopped biting and stepped away.

"That's what you get for saying you don't have a sweetheart, Steve," she said, laughing at me. "Everybody has a sweetheart—or wants one. What are you going to do about it now?"

Guthry noisily pushed his chair from the table and got to his feet. He was looking straight at Aunt Rosemary without saying a word to her.

"Come on, Steve," he told me with a sweep of his arm. "It's late. It's time for us to go."

Aunt Rosemary put her arms around Guthry and kissed him for a long time until he began stroking her up and down her back. After that, with her arms still around his neck, she turned her head and looked at me.

"Don't worry, Steve. I'll have everything all arranged for you when you get back. There are a lot of pretty girls in town at just the right age for you and you can have a date with one right after another till you find one you like best. Of course, all of them are nice girls—I wouldn't think of any other kind for you. Which is your favorite—blonde or brunet? And about fifteen or sixteen years old? What else?"

Guthry gave her a pat on the back that made her squirm and wiggle as he walked away.

"Don't get his mind on other things, Rosemary," he told her. "Right now we're going fishing and there'll be plenty of time for him to think about girls when we get back. When men go fishing, anything about girls is too distracting for such a serious business."

He pushed me toward the door.

"It's already getting to be daylight outside. Let's be going, Steve. We want to make an early start."

Aunt Rosemary came to the door and waved to us. As I looked back, the opening of her nightgown was even wider than it had been when we were eating breakfast.

"Rosemary," Guthry called to her sternly, "you be sure to get down to the store and open it up at eight o'clock every morning while we're away—well, by eight-thirty, anyhow. And don't you listen to those fast-talking traveling salesmen. I don't want you to sign an order for as much as a five-cent flyswatter while I'm gone. Tell those salesmen to get out of town. Now, remember that, Rosemary."

"Yes, Guthry. I'll remember. I know all about handling traveling salesmen, don't I?"

The sun was still not up when we left the house, but a reddish glow was coloring the gray sky in the east and the large white houses on both sides of Glenwood Street were already beginning to gleam in the early morning light. A heavy dew had covered everything during the night and the wide green lawns were wet with it and drops of water occasionally splashed on us as we walked on the graveled path under the oak trees on the way downtown.

It was seven blocks from Guthry's house to the hardware store and we got to the vacant lot at the rear of the building just as the sun was coming up behind the Illinois Central Railroad depot. We had seen nobody on the street, not even when we walked through the courthouse square, but Duke Hopkins had got there first and was energetically tramping down some of the bushy pigweeds that grew knee-high near the back door of the store.

Duke was a tall light-skin Negro about twenty-two or twenty-three years old with rounded muscles and an erect posture of body. Instead of being black and kinky, his hair was dark brown and wavy. He had a few scattered freckles high on his cheeks and his eyes were almost blue in color. He was wearing a white cotton shirt and gray cotton pants that had freshly ironed creases in them and had on a peaked, blue-stripe, cotton cloth cap of the kind worn by engineers, firemen, brakemen, and other people working on the railroad.

It was the first time I had seen Duke Hopkins, but Guthry had told me something about him the night before. He had been living in Unionville for the past two years since coming there to teach geography and history at the Negro grade school. However, the school salary was so small, even though he was not married and did not have a family to support, that he had rented space for a one-chair barbershop in a poolroom on

Prospect Avenue in the Negro section of town and hoped to earn enough extra money on weekends and during the summer to help pay for his living.

Duke had told Guthry that he could probably make a much better living if he stopped teaching school altogether and found a different kind of job, but that he liked teaching geography and history to young people—geography in particular—and wanted to keep on even if he did have to do part-time barbering or something else in order to be a schoolteacher. He had graduated from a Negro high school and had attended a Negro teachers' institute in Kentucky. He had learned the trade of barbering while in high school and that had made it possible for him to work his way through the teachers' institute.

2

GUTHRY HAD UNLOCKED the back door of the hardware store and, after moving most of the camping supplies outside on the loading platform, the three of us had been waiting for a quarter of an hour or longer when Troy Pickett finally got there and backed his truck up to the platform.

It was a much-used truck with a noisy engine and the body sagged on one side as though some of the springs had been broken by being overloaded with heavy freight. Originally it had been a flat-bed truck and Troy had made an all-weather van of it by building a wooden frame on it and covering it with sheets of tin roofing. He had painted the whole truck bright blue in color and by that time much of the paint had flaked off and left streaks of rusty tin that looked like splatters of red clay.

When Troy got out of the truck, he came toward us at the platform with a friendly wave of his hand. He had on the same droopy, rain-stained, sun-browned straw hat and an old dingy brown shirt that looked as if it had been worn without washing for many days and was wearing a pair of ripped overalls with dried yellow mud caked on the legs. He had not shaved that morning, or the day before, and his face was covered with a yellowish stubble.

"I'm a sonofabitch!" he called out, smiling broadly. "I'm late—I had an argument with my old woman. It's sure-God good to get away from all that nagging. How in hell do other married men stand it, Guthry? You're a married man—you ought to know."

"What did your wife say to you, Troy? Anything I haven't heard before?"

"I don't know about that, but if you ain't heard it yourself by now, then you just ain't lived long enough with a woman yet."

"What was it she said, Troy?"

Troy was still smiling good-naturedly. He had glanced only once at Duke Hopkins since getting there and still had not spoken to him.

"The same goddam thing she said the last time I went off fishing—and all the other times before that, too.

26

She's so pleased with her nagging that she won't change a word of it.

"She said, 'Troy Pickett, if you come back here stinking like you've been wallowing in a barrel of dead fish for a week like everytime before, you won't set foot inside this house. I'll run you out there in the back yard and make you strip off all your clothes down to your bare skin so I can slosh a bucket of kerosene all over you. Then I'll take a long-handle bristle brush and scrub you with lye and yellow soap clear down to the underside of your skin and still not sleep in the same bed with you for a month—if then.'

"That's how my old woman talks when I want to do something she don't like. She always ends up the same way when she's peeved—saying she won't get in the bed with me. Hell, she don't know it, but I've got other ways of going about doing that when I want it."

"What did you say when she told you that this time?" Guthry asked him.

"Nothing. Not a goddam thing. I'm used to it. I've learned it don't do no good to talk back to her. But I ain't quitting going fishing when I feel like it, neither. And when I want me a woman, and can't at home, I ain't particular. I just wait till sundown and go looking around and find me a high-yellow kind every time. And you can't do no better than that, nohow."

While we were loading the truck, Troy noticed the large wooden box that Duke Hopkins was taking with him. It was a homemade tackle box and carry-all with a hinged lid and a leather holding strap over the top.

27

It had been made with smooth white-pine boards from a shotgun-shell shipping case. The box was oblong in shape and would hold as much as an ordinary suitcase. Duke had lettered his name on it with a red-hot iron poker.

Troy slowly spelled aloud Duke's name letter-by-letter.

"What you got in that big box, boy?" Troy said to him then. "What's it for?"

"Mister Troy, it's just to carry some hooks and lines—and other things."

"And you need a whopping big box for only that? What other things you got in it, boy?"

"My razor and brush and some soap—and so on, Mister Troy."

Troy came closer, walking in a circle around the box and inspecting it curiously. And when he stopped, he gave it a hard kick.

"Why do you want to go to all the bother to shave yourself down there on the island for? You think that'll make you pretty-looking?"

"But, Mister Troy—" Duke tried to explain.

"Shut up—I haven't finished talking yet," Troy told him. "You can let your bristles grow out like everybody else does—nobody goes down there to look pretty. You think you'll look prettier than white people? What more you got inside that box, boy? A mirror to hold up to see how pretty you think you are?"

Before Duke could say anything, Troy flipped open the lid of the box.

On top of everything were several books. One of them was a large, square-shaped fifth-grade geography textbook with a map of the United States stamped on the cover in various colors. Another book was a small dictionary with a worn-out cover and ragged edges.

"I'm a sonofabitch!" Troy exclaimed with a short laugh. He kicked the box and then stepped backward to regard it with a scornful wrinkling of his face. "An educated nigger! Now ain't that something! You stand still and don't move so I can get a good look at you. I've heard of educated niggers but I never expected to see one this close before. It's a big treat for me. Say something educated, boy. I want to hear what an educated nigger talks like."

Duke grinned briefly. "Mister Troy, I don't know exactly what to say about that. I don't pretend to—"

"You're trying to be bashful about it, huh? Then tell me how come an educated nigger wants to go off fishing with white people. Is that because you think you're as good as white people? Maybe you know what to say about that."

"Well, I guess I'm just like anybody else, Mister Troy, when it comes to fishing."

"The hell you say! You're not like me, by God! I'm all-white—and you're half-assed black and half-assed white! But you're nothing but a nigger bastard no matter what and don't you forget it!"

"I don't pretend to be anything but what I am, Mister Troy."

"Shut up and quit that talking back to me!"

Nearly everything on the platform had been loaded by then and Guthry said we were wasting time and ought to be leaving right away.

It was almost seven o'clock and some people were already coming downtown on the way to their jobs. The sun was warm and bright by that time and the sky was clear and blue except for a few small flecks of white clouds over the southern horizon. The only sounds that early in the morning were coming from the Illinois Central Railroad freight yards two blocks away where a chuffing steam engine was coupling boxcars with a clanging noise.

Troy started walking around his truck and taking a last look to see if the tires were standing up well with such a heavy load. That was when two of the men who had tried to persuade Guthry the day before to let them go along with us came into the vacant lot from the street.

"Hey, Guthry Henderson!" one of the men called out. "When it starts raining down there on the island, are you going to let that nigger sleep in the same tent with you?"

Guthry ignored them as though not having heard a word of what had been said.

"That ain't the way it is," the other man said loudly. "Guthry Henderson wouldn't do that. But I know what Guthry's up to—he thinks he's got a secret scheme about it."

"What's Guthry's secret, George?"

"As soon as he gets a few miles out of sight of town and sees what he wants, he's going to swap off that nigger boy for a good-looking nigger gal to take with him. Then he'll pray for rain down there on the island every night so he'll have a good excuse to be real kindhearted and tell her to come inside the tent and not stay outside and get all wet in the rain. Guthry Henderson is a fine kindhearted man when it comes to something like that—except for when he won't let his real white friends go along fishing with him. Ain't that right, Guthry?"

"Go to hell!" Guthry told them.

"Now, Guthry, don't go and get all touchy and cranky. Your wife won't never know nothing about it. You can trust me not to spread tales about it around town. That wouldn't be like me. I'm always loyal to my good friends like you no matter how mean and selfish you are about not letting me and George go along with you. You go on down the road and keep your eyes open for a good-looking high-yellow gal to swap off that ugly old nigger boy for."

3

GUTHRY GOT INTO THE FRONT SEAT to ride beside Troy. Duke and I climbed into the back of the truck and sat down on the pile of sleeping quilts.

Before starting the engine, however, Troy came to the back of the truck again and told us to keep the big brown croker sack from bouncing around on the hard floor and breaking the bourbon bottles he was taking down to the river.

"You listen to me, boy," he said, pointing his finger at Duke. "Don't you let none of that good red whiskey break open and spill out and go to waste. You treat that sack like it was full of fresh-laid eggs. You hear? If you take good care of it and don't let none spill, I might let you have a little drink of it down on the island now and then. I don't want to get down there and find some of them bottles broken and be short of good red whiskey all that time. That'd spoil the whole trip for me and make me want to beat a hole in your hide."

"I'll do my best, Mister Troy," Duke said, moving the heavy sack of bottles and putting it beside him on top of the quilts. "I know how you feel about it."

"If you keep all them bottles from getting broken," he said as he walked away, "maybe it'll prove being an educated nigger is good for something, anyhow."

When we were leaving the weedy lot at the rear of the hardware store, the two men who were being left behind picked up some chips and sticks from the ground and tossed them at us. Most of them hit the tin covering on the truck and made a rattling noise until we got to the street and out of reach. They had been shouting at Guthry, too, but the noise of the truck engine was so loud that we could not hear what it was they were saying.

After crossing the railroad tracks and then going along Crockett Street past a few stores and some small houses for several blocks, we got to the end of the pavement at the city limits.

The narrow dirt road began abruptly with a loud thump of the wheels and a big bounce of the truck and we were soon raising a cloud of yellow dust behind us. Unlike the present-day wide and smooth black-top highway, which is bridged and well-drained, and which can be easily traveled in automobile or truck all the way from Unionville to the Mississippi River in an hour or less, at that time the road was dusty and rutted in dry weather and slippery and miry after the slightest rainfall. In those early days, there were many creeks without bridges that had to be forded and frequent mud holes that never dried up completely the year around. And when there was flooding after a prolonged summer thunderstorm, the road was sometimes impassable for several days or even a week at a time.

Troy Pickett's old truck could go no faster than twelve or fifteen miles an hour between creeks and mud holes, but it was not long until we had left the clay hills behind us and were deep in the low country with cornfields and cowpastures on both sides of the road and which was bordered by dense thickets of wild blackberry bushes and sassafras saplings and cottonwoods.

The gray field rabbits, after leisurely crossing the road, stopped and watched us curiously; and the crows, perching on fence posts, cawed and cawed incessantly. Occasionally there was a sizable farmhouse of a white landowner that had a hayloft barn and a corncrib and a milking shed behind it. However, most of the dwellings along the road were one- or two-room, unpainted, Negro tenant cabins where numerous children of various ages in ragged overalls and skimpy dresses stopped playing in the yards and ditches and came to the roadside to look at us as we passed. The older boys and girls merely stood and stared at us as we went by, but the younger children, shouting gleefully and jumping up and down with excitement, waved to us until we were out of sight around a curve of the road. Their fathers were plowing in the fields and their mothers, along with some of the older girls, were hoeing cotton and corn nearby.

"What kind of house do you live in down there in Memphis, Steve?" Duke asked me as we looked at the tenant cabins we were passing. "I like to think about the kind of houses where people live—but I sure don't like the looks of the kind of shacks along this road that colored people live in. And I don't like the looks of a lot of them for the colored in Unionville, either. There sure is a lot of difference between those big white houses on Glenwood Street and the tumbled-down shacks on Prospect Avenue. Do you live in a big house or a little house in Memphis, Steve?"

I told Duke it was a medium-size, one-story, yellow-color house with a narrow front porch and an even smaller back porch. Like all the other houses on Penny-ton Street, it had been built close to the sidewalk and had only enough space behind it and the alley for a wood-and-coal shed. The houses on each side of it were so close that anybody could lean out and slam the blinds on the neighbors' windows.

When Duke said he wanted to know more about my neighborhood in Memphis, I told him that nearly all the men who lived on Pennyton Street, which was five blocks long and zigzagged like many of the southside streets, worked at a guano bagging plant or at a nearby cotton compress plant. When a man walked along the street on his way home from work in the late afternoon, unless he happened to be one of the few who had a different kind of job somewhere else in Memphis, he would either be shedding cotton lint from his clothes or he would smell like a guano fertilizer factory.

Duke opened his tackle box and took out the geography textbook. He turned the pages carefully until he found one of the maps. He studied it for a long time while we bounced with each lurch of the truck on the rough road.

"I want to go down to Memphis one of these days soon," he said presently, holding his finger at a place on the map while he gazed down the road behind us. "It must be a real big city—a lot bigger than Paducah. If I could get me a teaching job in a colored school down in Memphis—but I'd have to go to the teachers' institute some more first. I've only studied there for one year so far and that might not be enough for teaching in a big city like Memphis. I don't want to stay in Unionville, and have to do barbering, too, all my life. And I wouldn't want to go to Memphis and have to make out a living barbering there on the side, either. I want to be a real schoolteacher—the kind who can be a teacher anywhere he wants to. If I can get to be that, then I can go around and learn more about geography first-hand. I could go up and down and all over the country— Chicago, Cincinnati, St. Louis, Memphis, New Orleans. Just look at all the places on this map! Just think of that! This sure is a handsome big country to roam around in! It makes me feel good just to be alive in it!"

THREE

1

WE FORDED three sandy-bottom creeks that morning with no trouble at all and did not get stuck in the mud until we came to a quagmire of silt covering the roadway and overflowing the ditches for a distance as long as a city block.

The silt, which was gray topsoil that had been washed from a plowed field by a heavy rain, was as slick and mushy as wet cement. When Duke got out of the truck and saw the whole quagmire, he said it looked to him as if somebody had come along and dumped a thousand barrels of chicken gravy on the road. Since we had no chains to put on the rear wheels when the truck sank axle-deep in the mud, we had to look for a split-rail fence to get some long poles to pry up the wheels so we could stuff brush and limbs under them.

Everybody except Troy Pickett, who stayed in the front seat yelling out and telling us what to do, was soaking wet and muddy up to the knees by the time we could push the truck out of the miry silt to firm ground and our shirts and faces had been splattered with the gray mud by the spinning rear wheels.

It took us more than an hour to get out of the sink hole and by then it was already noon and we were still six or seven miles from Little Dipper Landing where we were going to rent a skiff to get to Summertime Island.

All of us were hungry by that time. Troy wanted to open some of the cans of baked beans, but Guthry said there was a store at a fork of the road only half a mile away and that we could buy something to eat there and save the baked beans to eat on the island in case we could not catch any catfish right away.

This was when Troy said he could stand going hungry for a little while longer but did not have to go thirsty when there was plenty of red whisky to drink. He got a bottle of bourbon from the croker sack and took it to the front seat with him.

When we got to the small store at the fork of the road—a settlement called Happiness—Troy took another drink from the bottle before getting out of the truck and said he would not even mind going hungry for a while longer after that. There were several two-room tenant houses within sight, and a few scattered persimmon trees and cottonwoods, and everywhere else were flat fields of cotton and corn and fenced cowpastures. The only people we saw were two elderly Negro men sitting on a bench in the shade of a tall cottonwood tree in front of the store. They stood up, mumbling indistinctly, and took off their hats as we walked past them.

The name of the owner of the store was Hugh Huff-man—both his name and Happiness, Tennessee, were lettered in faded blue paint across the top of the dash-board front of the tin-roofed building—and he was alone when we went inside. Hugh Huffman was a large, red-faced man about fifty years old with a bulging stomach that overlapped the top of his pants and swayed from side to side when he moved. He had on a gray-tinted white shirt that looked as if it had been washed recently but not ironed.

There was a meager stock of merchandise in the store—being mostly bolts of gingham cloth and kegs of nails and stacks of overalls and a few cans of potted ham and sock-eye salmon—but there was a large forty-pound round of daisy cheese covered with a ragged gray cloth to keep the flies off and plenty of soda crackers to eat with it. Guthry put some money on the counter and said that we wanted four big chunks of cheese and a box of crackers for everybody.

As soon as the wedges of the yellow cheese were cut from the round and handed to us on sheets of brown wrapping paper, we began eating right away.

"Now hold on here!" the storekeeper said in a loud rough tone, coming from behind the counter and waving the cheese knife at us. "Wait just a minute! I don't allow nothing like this!"

"What's the matter?" Guthry asked him, chewing a mouthful of cheese and crackers. "We're hungry and I've paid you for everything."

"I know you did—I'm not talking about that. I took your money and gave you the change."

"Then what's wrong?"

"I'll tell you what's wrong. I don't know who you folks are or where you came from or what you're up to and it makes no difference to me. But I'm Hugh Huffman and everybody around here knows I don't allow no blacks to come in my store and act like whites. Blacks can buy all they've got the money to pay for, but after that they've got to leave my store and go outside, and I don't care if it's cold and sleeting out there, neither. I sure wouldn't allow none of them to stand around in here and eat in front of me like white people. Now, get that nigger out of my store and hurry up about it."

He pointed the cheese knife at Duke Hopkins. Duke moved backward toward the door.

"Don't you chew one more time in front of me, nigger!"

"It's all right," Guthry said, taking another bite of daisy cheese. "Don't bother him. He's going fishing with us and we brought him in here to get something to eat. If he can go fishing with us, he can eat with us. Let him finish his cheese and crackers. He's hungry like the rest of us. Leave him alone."

The storekeeper banged the cheese knife on the counter so hard that it rattled some of the cans of ham and salmon on the shelves.

"You can take him fishing with you—and all the way to hell, too—if you want to. That's your business. But he ain't going to stand here in my store and eat in front of me. That's my business. You go outside and ask the first black you see and he'll tell you the same thing about me. All the blacks around here know about me. Now, get that nigger out of here in a hurry like I said or I'll take after him and run him out myself."

"Cut him off another slice of that cheese," Guthry said, pointing at Duke. "This is just about the best cheese I've tasted in a long time."

Throwing down the cheese knife, the storekeeper went behind the counter and picked up an ax handle. It was about three feet long and one end of it had been weighted with a thick iron band. Holding it above his head and swinging it threateningly, he went toward Duke. Duke quickly moved farther away.

Troy stepped between them.

"Don't do anything about me, Mister Troy," Duke called to him. "I'm getting out of here."

"Shut up!" Troy yelled back. "Don't you open your mouth to tell me what not to do!"

He slapped his hand on the storekeeper's bulging stomach and shoved him backward against the counter.

"I'm a sonofabitch!" Troy said. "I didn't come in here to get in a fist fight about a nigger, but if you want one, it suits me fine and by God I'll give it to you. And you couldn't pick out anybody better than me to give it to you, neither. I don't like the way you cut that hunk of cheese for me, anyhow. When I want a piece of cheese, I want it cut nice and slick and not all ragged and crumbly like you done. Don't you know nobody wants to eat a slice of cheese if it ain't cut nice and slick and not all crumbly and falling to pieces? Don't you know nothing?"

"You're drunk," Hugh Huffman said. "I could tell that by looking at you when you came in here. And I can smell whiskey all over you now. You're stinking drunk. A white man wouldn't take up for a nigger like you're doing if he wasn't. You'd be ashamed of yourself to let anybody see you act like a nigger-loving white man if you was sober. Now get yourself out of my store in a big hurry and sober up and go on somewhere else about your business."

By that time, Duke had left the store and gone outside to wait for us.

"Nobody calls me a nigger-lover and don't get hurt!" Troy said. "Drunk or sober or in between—that's something I'm goddam particular about and don't take from nobody. I'll learn you! I'm Troy Pickett, by God!"

"You can be the bastard son of Jesus Christ for all I care—"

His fists gripped tightly and crouching forward, Troy first butted Hugh Huffman's bulging belly and then began pounding it with all his might.

Guthry tried to stop the fighting, but, before he could get a grip on Troy's arm and pull him away, the store-keeper had been shoved against the shelves and was being beaten on the head and shoulders with the weighted ax handle. With blood running down his face, he slumped to the floor out of sight behind the counter. Troy was reaching for the cheese knife when Guthry was able to pull him away and drag him out of the store.

2

THE TWO ELDERLY NEGRO MEN had got up from the bench under the cottonwood tree and were watching Guthry and Troy leave the store and go toward the truck.

"Don't stand there like that and look at me with your goddam hats on your head!" Troy yelled at them. "Don't you know nothing?"

They quickly took off their hats and bowed their heads as he walked past them.

"Just because I'm a stranger don't you two blacks never forget I'm a white man," he told them.

"Yes, sir, boss," both of them were quick to say.

When Troy saw Duke standing beside the truck, he jerked his arm from Guthry's grip.

"Look here, boy," he said to Duke. "I'm going to tell you something and you'd better listen to what I say. Don't you never go around Unionville or nowhere else telling people I took up for you and got in a scrap about it. I don't never want that known about me. Now, just to prove to you it didn't mean a goddam thing, I'm going to show you. Bend over!"

"Why do you want me to do that, Mister Troy?" he asked, laughing a little. "What's it for? I sure appreciate what you did—"

"Quit talking and do like I told you. That'll show you why. Now bend over and grab your ankles."

"I wish you'd tell me something—"

"Shut up and do like I said."

Duke hesitated for a moment, as if he might continue to protest, before turning around and bending forward. He leaned over only far enough to touch his knees with his hands and that was when Troy kicked him lightly on the seat of his pants.

Duke immediately straightened up and turned around to look at Troy with a perplexed expression.

"Now you see what I mean, boy," Troy said, grinning as he spoke. "Now you know why. That puts you in your place. We're right back where we started from and going to stay. You're a black bastard and I'm a white sonofabitch. Black and white—black and white— just exactly like we both got born and are going to keep on. And don't you never forget it around me, neither. If you get bigheaded and try to forget it, I'll be right there to kick it back in your mind. Now grab your pecker and climb in that truck, boy. It's getting late and I want to get down to the river in the daylight before it gets too scary after dark."

When we left Hugh Huffman's store, we took the right-hand fork of the road that Guthry had said went all the way down to Little Dipper Landing at the river. We had gone only a short distance westward along the narrow dirt-track road when we passed an abandoned one-room schoolhouse with broken windows. Next to it was a small unpainted church with an adjoining grave-yard where a few gray-green mossy tombstone slabs were barely visible above a rank growth of weeds.

After going about half a mile beyond the Happiness church and graveyard, the flat fields of corn and cotton and the cowpastures were suddenly left behind and the narrow road began winding downhill where the land was gully-washed and barren and only occasionally had scattered clumps of stunted thickets and briars clinging to it. Without houses and farm buildings anywhere within sight, it was like a wasteland where people had never wanted to live.

Neither Duke nor I had said anything since leaving Hugh Huffman's store until he asked me how I would feel if a Negro man told me to bend over and be kicked. I had been thinking about what Troy Pickett had done, too, and wondering how I would have felt if I were a Negro and had been kicked by a white man.

"Maybe when you're not colored you don't know how you'd feel about that," he said.

The first thing I said was that I would never want to be kicked like that by anybody, Negro or white, whether playfully or not. However, as soon as I had said that, I recalled very clearly playing a game with Negro and white playmates in Memphis when I was about eight years old. When I told Duke about it, he wanted to know what the rules were and how the game was played.

As I remembered it, I told him, it was a choose-up game similar to one-eyed-cat baseball with only two bases instead of four and with five, six, or seven Negro and white boys on both teams and we played at a large vacant lot on Saturdays and in the late afternoon of schooldays when it was not raining or too cold in winter. Actually, the vacant lot, which was three blocks from where I lived on Pennyton Street, was a grassy field of several acres separating a Negro settlement and a white residential section and a halfway meetingplace for young boys of both neighborhoods.

At the end of every game, which took anywhere from twenty minutes to half an hour to play, the boys on the winning team had the privilege of playfully kicking the boys on the losing team. Being of that age, and at that time, nobody ever became angry and started a fight when he was playfully kicked by a boy of a different color, since we had made the rules ourselves and it was part of the game, and the losers always strived harder the next time to be the winning team and do the kicking. One of the older boys always appointed himself the captain of a team and each captain always wanted to choose the best players, Negro or white, in order to have the winning team. And if two boys ever got into a quarrel while we were playing, they had to go to the other side of the field to wrestle or fight so we could finish the game.

When I had finished telling Duke about Negro and white boys between seven and ten years old playfully kicking one another at that time in Memphis, he said he remembered a similar kind of baseball game Negro and white boys played in Paducah when he was very young.

"We had a lot of different names for the kind of baseball we played," he said, "because it all depended on how many boys wanted to play on a team—sometimes only four or five, sometimes ten or twelve.

"Anyway, that's exactly what I thought about when Mister Troy kicked me at the store a little while ago.

He didn't kick me hard enough to hurt—it was so light I hardly felt it—and I didn't have it in mind to turn around and kick him. It was more like those games we've been talking about. It makes me think a lot of white men want to be friendly if they could let themselves and not always wanting to do something mean to colored people.

"The trouble is that so far in my life I haven't seen enough of that kind of white man to make much difference. Everywhere I go it's just like it got to be after a while in Kentucky when I started growing up. The white boys turned on us when they got to be ten or eleven years old and started calling us ugly names and throwing rocks and chasing us away from where we'd been playing together. Our parents told us to keep away from the white boys after that and stay in our place to keep out of trouble. And it's been that way ever since, too. Stay in your place, black boy! Stay in your place!

"I wouldn't mind staying in my place," Duke said after thinking about it for a moment, "if they'd let me look around and choose it myself instead of it always being where the white people say it's got to be—right down on the bottom of the trash pile. I'd go somewhere in this big country and make my place a fine college where I could study and learn as much as a white student so I could get to be a real professor—not just a half-educated teacher in a five-grade shanty schoolhouse for the colored like it is now. That's my big ambition in life—getting a full education and then being Professor Duke Hopkins in a big college or university. If I could do that, I'd be so proud of myself that I'd change my

name from being just ordinary and be Professor
Paducah Hopkins. Wouldn't that be something! And
with a name like that—Professor Paducah Hopkins—
they'd never tramp me back down to the bottom of
any trash pile and keep me there."

The brakes had been squeaking all the way down
the steep slope from the top of the bluff and the truck
had been lurching and tossing us around on the winding road. Then suddenly we reached the flat marshy
ground where the road was smooth and straight. On
both sides were tall green willows and cottonwoods and
tangled growth of vines and bushes and wildflowers.

It was late in the afternoon then with the sun already low over the treetops and the long shadows were
becoming dim in the warm misty dampness of the
marsh.

3

WHEN WE REACHED the Little Dipper boat landing on
the mud flat, all of us got out and walked around to
stretch the stiffness out of our legs after being cramped
in the truck for most of the day. In addition to the boat
landing, which was a log skid about six feet wide and
thirty or forty feet long and worn smooth by the flat-
bottom skiffs being pulled on shore to keep them safe
from swamping in stormy weather, there was an open-
sided shed sheltering a partly built skiff on sawhorses.

On a grassy hummock behind the shed and high

enough to be above ordinary flood stage, there was a tin-roofed dwelling that had several rooms and a screened porch all the way across the front of the house. We could see several skiffs on the mud bank above the skid and there was smoke coming from the kitchen chimney. However, there was nobody within sight and the only sound was the loud croaking of frogs in the marsh and along the reedy edge of the water.

Guthry told us to wait where we were while he went up to the house on the hummock to talk to Clyde Owens, who lived there and rented skiffs to fishermen, and to find out which one we would be using.

It was still daylight in the clearing by the water, but a few mosquitoes were already humming around us and Duke and I slapped at them while we waited. Troy said the smell of red whiskey would keep any mosquito from getting close enough to bite and he took a big drink of bourbon and then rubbed some more of it on his face and neck and over the backs of his hands.

When Guthry got to the top of the hummock, which was a long mound of soft earth about twenty feet high, he stopped and called Clyde Owens. In a few moments Clyde came out of the house, loudly slamming the screen door behind him, and came down to the mud flat with Guthry.

"How you folks today?" Clyde said genially, shaking hands with everybody except Duke Hopkins.

He paused momentarily and stared curiously at Duke as if unaccustomed to seeing a Negro with such light skin and brownish straight hair.

"Glad to meet you—glad to know you," he said then.

"Don't see people down here at Little Dipper much often. Always glad to see anybody. It gets lonesome down here. You folks got fishing on your mind, huh? Well, there's plenty of cat out there to take—if you're smart enough to go about it their way and don't waste their time and yours trying to be scientific about it. If you're not going to put out a trotline—well, then you might as well turn right around and go back home now." He shook his head firmly from side to side as if giving us a final warning. "And if you're figuring on doing pole-fishing at Summertime Island, I can tell you right now all you'll get is some messy carp for your trouble."

Clyde Owens was a man of medium height and who appeared to be between forty-five and fifty years old and was wearing baggy tan cotton pants and a faded blue cotton shirt. He had on mud-caked heavy brogans without socks. His broad smiling face had been creased by sun and rain and thick locks of sun-bleached reddish hair tumbled over his forehead and down the back of his neck.

"But let me tell you folks something else," he said with a serious shaking of his head. "You'd be making a mighty late start to get over to Summertime before dark. I wouldn't want to let myself row over there now and try to set up camp this late in the dark if I was a stranger here. You don't have no city electric lights over there, for one thing. And besides, a new current sprang up in the middle of that backwater slough about a month ago when the river flooded and almost made a new main channel. The way it is now it takes some mighty hard rowing to get across that swift water and not get carried down past the island and way-to-hell-and-gone downriver before you can help yourself. I wouldn't want none of my boats to end up somewhere down past Memphis snagged and splintered on a hickory stump."

"There's plenty of daylight left," Guthry told him, anxious to get started. He began walking nervously up and down on the mud flat. "We've spent all day getting here from Unionville and we want to make it to the island now so we can get in some fishing the first thing in the morning. That's what we came here for— fishing and nothing else—and don't want to waste a minute. Just show us the skiff you're going to rent us so we can load up and go."

"Well, there's nothing else to do on that island except fishing—unless you take along some frisky women and good whiskey."

"You don't look to me like somebody who knows much about women and whiskey," Troy told him. "I don't see no place around this god-forsaken hole to find either one."

With a glowering glance at Troy, Clyde turned and walked away.

We followed Clyde along the mud flat to the skid where he pointed to two ten-foot skiffs on the bank. The boats were mud-stained and water-warped and the two oarlocks on each of them had broken loose and then been fastened to the splintered wood with rusty wire.

Guthry shook his head as soon as he saw them.

"That won't do, Clyde. I wouldn't start out across a horse pond with one of those. We want a good solid-bottom fifteen-footer."

"Nope," Clyde said flatly. "Not mine, you won't. I wouldn't risk it. You take those two little ones—or you don't take nothing. If they don't come back, I wouldn't be out much."

Troy came closer, pushing Guthry aside.

"You talk mighty goddam big for a river rat who don't even have a tail to drag behind you," he said to Clyde. "We know what we want. And if you know what's good for you, you'll shut up and pull that big boat down to the water like we want it."

"And you can shut up and do it fast—or you won't get no boat at all!"

Guthry tried to pull Troy away.

"Let me take care of this, Troy," he said calmly. "We don't want any trouble."

Troy jerked his arm from Guthry's grip.

"If you don't skid that goddam boat down to the water like we want it," he shouted at Clyde, "I'll push it off myself and throw you in the river and stomp you down on the bottom of it!"

"You won't do nothing but slobber out of your mouth! Now get the hell away from here and go back where you came from!"

"I'm a sonofabitch!" Troy yelled at him.

"You look like a sonofabitch!"

"Don't you call me that!"

"What do you want to be—a sonofabitching bastard?"

Guthry and Duke got between them and held them apart. Troy drew back his fist and hit Duke.

There was a slamming of the screen door at the house on the hummock and somebody came running toward us.

"Papa! Papa! What's the matter?"

A girl about seventeen years old, brushing her blond hair from her face, had come within a few yards of us. With a frightened look, she stood there clutching her blue cotton dress over her chest. She was bare-legged and wearing tennis shoes and was tall and slender with wide full lips that quivered as she watched us.

"What's the trouble about, Papa?" she called out excitedly.

"Betty, run back to the house and bring me my gun," Clyde told her. "Hurry up! Don't waste time!"

"Please don't get in a fight, Papa!"

"You go get me my gun like I told you!"

"Come on back to the house—please, Papa!"

"Do like I told you, Betty! Quit wasting time!"

"Oh, please, Papa!" she begged as she left and ran toward the house.

Troy turned and watched her interestedly until she had gone out of sight.

"You've got a mighty pretty daughter," he said to Clyde with a friendly smile as if he had never been angry at all. "I noticed that right away. She sure is a real good-looking girl. It's been a long time since I've seen one as pretty as she is."

Clyde was grimly silent.

53

"Everybody here got a little too excited," Troy said then, slapping his hand on Clyde's shoulder. "That's all it was. There's no real trouble about nothing."

Betty came running back with a pistol and handed it to her father. She stood aside then, watching fearfully.

"When two people like us meet up the first time," Troy said earnestly, "it always takes a little while to get acquainted. I've noticed that all my life. Haven't you, too, Clyde? We can be good friends from now on, can't we, Clyde? Ain't that right, Clyde?"

"I ain't saying if I want to or not. Anyhow, you still got to take those two little skiffs—or none at all."

"That suits fine," Troy said agreeably, looking at the girl while he was talking. She smiled at him slightly and folded her arms tightly under her breasts. "Nothing suits better, Clyde. That big boat wouldn't hold all four of us and all the stuff we've got to take to the island, anyway. We need two of them—just like you said. Don't we, Guthry? Ain't that right, Guthry? Don't you say so, Guthry? Huh?"

"Come on," Guthry said, motioning to Duke and me. "Let's hurry up and move our things to those skiffs so we can get across the water to the island before it's real dark."

FOUR

1

As SOON as we could carry all our camping supplies from the truck and load them on both skiffs, we were ready to leave Little Dipper and start rowing across the backwater to Summertime Island.

However, Troy Pickett said he had left something important in the truck and had to go back to get it. Clyde Owens had gone off somewhere out of sight and Betty was standing outside the screen door at the house on the hummock where she could watch us.

When Troy went back to the truck, not even trying to hurry, Guthry was so provoked that he got into one of the skiffs, set the oarlocks, and told me to push it off the mud bank and jump aboard because he was not going to waste any more time when there was so little daylight left.

We left Duke, wide-eyed with anxiety, standing beside the other skiff at the landing.

"What about me, Mister Guthry?" he called to us as Guthry began pulling on the oars. "Don't go off and leave me behind at this strange place!"

"This skiff is already loaded down with all it'll hold. One more in here would swamp it for sure. You'll have to wait for Troy."

"Yeh, I know, but suppose he's got a notion to stay here all night where that girl is—he's got something like that in mind. I noticed that about him. I don't want to be left here and miss all the fishing."

"Give him a little time to get in trouble, Duke. Then if he gets shot and fails to show up after a while, start rowing across to the island. And when you get to that swift current Clyde Owens told us about, keep the boat headed sort of kitty-cornered and row like hell. You'll land on the island all right if you do that."

"Yeh, I know, but which way is kitty-cornered out there in that water in the dark?"

"Sort of half-sideways like you'd be headed up north to Chicago but going out west to Kansas City too at the same time."

"Yeh, I know, but how can I tell which direction that is?"

"Open up your geography book and look at the map."

"This's a scary fix to be in," we heard Duke say on the shore. "It's getting dark fast and I'll hardly know which way is straight up and which way is straight down when I get out there all by myself. I didn't know it'd be like this down here on the river when I said I wanted to come fishing. Right now I sure wish I could change my mind and not be here."

"It's too late to change your mind now," Guthry called across the water to him. "Anyway, you won't have any trouble, Duke. There'll be some starlight shining down soon for you to see by. Just remember what I said about rowing across the current kitty-cornered. But if you get lost out there, holler as loud as you can and I'll hear you and tell you what to do."

It was several moments before we heard Duke again.

"Mister Guthry!" he called anxiously.

"What do you want, Duke?"

"Are you sure nothing could happen to me?"

"Not if you holler loud enough."

"How far did you say it is over to that island?"

"Not much more than an eighth of a mile—in a straight line. But maybe a quarter-mile if you do a lot of zigzagging crossing that current."

It was nightfall by the time we got nearly halfway across the backwater. The moon had not come up yet, but a few of the brightest stars were already shining in the cloudless sky. It was a warm summer night with only a slight breeze from the south to ripple the water. Every once in a while Guthry turned around and looked to make sure he was rowing the skiff in a true course toward the dim outline of the island.

The current was not as strong at that particular time as Clyde Owens had warned it might be and we soon crossed it and were in calm water where limbs and other driftwood were floating all around us. That was when Guthry told me to take the oars and row the rest of the way. We changed seats, being careful not to tip the heavily loaded boat, and he sat on the narrow board at the stern and motioned with his hands from time to time so I could row in a straight course to the island.

The only sound was the dipping of the oars in the water until somewhere in the main channel of the river on the other side of the island there was a startling blast of the hoarse whistle of a river steamboat and after that the resounding echoes gradually faded into silence. It was a lonely place to be in the dark, even with Guthry in the boat, and I wondered how Duke was going to feel if he had to cross the backwater all by himself.

"We're almost there now, Steve," Guthry said presently. "I'm beginning to see the trees and brush on the island already. And I bet you're just as hungry as I am. I'm glad we brought along plenty of cans of pork-and-beans—they're going to taste mighty good to a hungry stomach. And we'll build a fire and make plenty of strong hot coffee to go with them. But then tomorrow we'll be eating fried catfish and that'll make the trip down here worthwhile. And that's what we came down here for—plenty of fried catfish."

He turned around and looked back at Little Dipper Landing. There was only a single light to be seen anywhere on shore and it was dim and barely twinkling over the water. That was when he asked me if I wish I'd stayed there instead of Troy Pickett. I knew he was talking about the good-looking girl we had seen there and I had been thinking about her too.

"Steve, I bet that girl would a lot rather for you to be there than Troy. He's an old man compared to how young she is and you're at just the right age for her. She must get awfully lonely staying there all the time without somebody like you around. But maybe she's so lonely that even Troy looks good to her. It wouldn't take you long to get friendly with her, would it? Her name is Betty, isn't it? That's what her father called her. You liked her looks, didn't you, Steve?"

I told him that I thought Betty was a very pretty girl and wanted to be friendly with somebody but that I would have been too afraid of her father to stay there and try to have a date with her.

"That's the trouble about being your age, Steve," he said sympathetically. "That's when you're all fired up and can't always do something about it. You see a girl like her and get a big urge for her and then before anything happens her father comes along and scares the hell out of you. I know all about it. I've been there. Many times when I was your age. It's something you never forget when you grow up, either. That's when you want to get skin-tight to a girl like all hell but can't do it no matter how willing she is when her old man is watching every move you make because he knows what you're after and he'll run you off every time before you can get under her dress. And what the hell! That's what it's all about. And if you can't get under her dress, you haven't gone anywhere.

"It's plain hell when you're at your age, Steve. You bet I haven't forgotten. You can go off and masturbate but that doesn't help for long because you bounce right back and want a girl more than ever. That's when you know only the real thing is going to satisfy you. So what then? You wouldn't want to get married when you're that young—you'd be a fool to do that. And what else can you do about it? I know. You go looking for a girl who's willing and knows what to do about privacy. And who's she? She's either a nice girl who'll accept candy or a bad girl who demands money. And whether they want candy or money, it's all the same if you get what you crave. So when you find out what they want, go ahead and give it to them and get what you're after.

"And here's something else, Steve. Don't take chances with any of them. You go to the drugstore first and say you want to buy some rubbers for the prevention of disease. That's the best insurance you can get to keep from getting what some of them will give you a dose of—clap or blue balls or God knows what else. Or having one of them tell you she's going to have a baby and that you've got to marry her or pay her big money. See what I mean?

"How did I get started talking like this, Steve? I know now. It was that girl back there at the boat landing. Well, there are some things you can talk about in the dark a lot better than you can in the daylight. Anyway, I don't know what you know about these things, but it won't do any harm to tell you all over again even if you've already heard it before. And I don't know what your dad has told you about girls and women, but I can say things in plain words that maybe he wouldn't say. A boy's father can be too embarrassed about it. That's the way my own dad was and I couldn't find out what I wanted to know for a long time. No matter how much your dad wants to help you, something keeps him from going far enough. And it's something you're too shy to ask your mother about, too. That's natural. And then if you ask other boys, they don't know any more than you do. Or they'll boast that they do and you could end up with more trouble than you can live with.

"Well that's the good thing about having an uncle— he can be a mighty good friend when it comes to things like that. I know about that. When I finally asked my own uncle a few questions, he knew exactly what was bothering me and he came right out with plain talk. That's when I wished I'd asked him a lot sooner. He spoke up and put me straight about a lot of things I needed to know.

"And so now that you're at your age, and get a big urge for a girl and want to get under her dress, I can be mighty understanding about it instead of saying— like some people would—that you shouldn't think about such things. That's a hell of a way to treat a boy your age. You can't keep from thinking about it no more than you can keep from feeling hungry when your belly is empty.

"I can tell you what'd happen if you listen to too much of that kind of talk—and start believing it. You could get so put off about women, and made shy of them, that you could end up with a bunch of boys and grown men who use each other for the same thing instead of being natural with girls and women. You keep that in mind, Steve. There's a lot of that going on wher-

ever you are—and don't you forget it. Go after a girl
every time, Steve. Don't let yourself get side-tracked.
You uncle says so."

2

GUTHRY, HAVING BEEN THERE BEFORE, knew exactly
where he wanted to land the skiff on Summertime Island and when we were a few boat-lengths away he
told me to row straight ahead. The grayish earth was
soft but not muddy where we beached the skiff and
beginning at the edge of the backwater there was a
wide clearing where trees and bushes had been cut
down by other fishermen for the campsite.

We had brought a lantern with us but did not light
it. Instead, Guthry scooped up some leaves and twigs
and kindled a fire right away in the middle of the clearing. The fire blazed up brightly and it was easy enough
after that to find plenty of dry driftwood to keep it
burning. In a few minutes the campfire had lighted
the clearing all the way to the edge of the backwater
where we had beached the skiff.

Birds of many colors were roosting in trees and bushes
all around us and we could hear them chirping and
fluttering their wings as if they had been awakened by
the light of sunrise. Now and then one of the birds,
aroused from sleep, would fly around us in a helter-
skelter way until it could find another perch in a tree.
There were cawing crows and whooing owls in the

taller trees, too, and we could see the big round eyes of some of the owls shining in the firelight.

Guthry said probably there were copperhead snakes and water moccasins that had got to the island on floating logs and stumps but that there was little danger of snakebites because they would go into hiding when they heard our voices and footsteps. He said there might even be a few rabbits and raccoons—and maybe a fox or two—that had come downstream on large planks and timbers during the spring floods. However, at night, it was too dark to see anything much beyond the clearing except for the shiny green leaves of the tall willows gleaming in the campfire.

We had unloaded some of the supplies from the skiff and had carried them to the clearing when we heard pistol shots across the backwater. There had been three shots fired in quick succession and then after the echoes had faded away the only sound to be heard was the gentle lapping of water on the skiff.

Guthry, looking at me with a solemn shaking of his head, smiled slightly.

"Well, dead or alive," he said slowly, "Troy Pickett asked for it if a man ever did. I could see it coming and the only thing that surprises me is that it took this long for it to happen. Clyde Owens was itching to shoot somebody as soon as he got his hand on that pistol. Troy knew that. Looks like he would've had better sense than stay there and risk fooling around with that girl. He could've waited a few days to get back to Unionville for what he wanted."

I told Guthry that I was glad he had not left me at the boat landing to be shot three times.

"Now, Steve, who would want to shoot an innocent young boy just because he'd been caught holding hands with a girl?"

We looked across the backwater in the darkness and listened to hear if any more shots were fired. There was silence everywhere and all we could see was the dim twinkling light on the shore.

"Well, that must've been the end of the shooting— and maybe the end of Troy, too," Guthry said. "And if the worst did happen to Troy Pickett, it's going to be up to me to tell his wife. That's something I hate to have to do. I'd have to tell her the whole truth about it, because the sheriff will find out how it happened and it would all come out in court, anyway. If a man gets drunk and picks a fight or is caught cheating in a poker game—that's something else. But when a married man gets shot for fooling around with another woman—or if an outside man gets shot for fooling around with a married woman—"

Guthry started walking to the campfire in the middle of the clearing.

"Come on, Steve," he called to me. "Let's boil some coffee and open up some pork-and-beans. I'm hungry as hell. And I bet you are, too. It's been a long time since we had that bite of cheese and crackers back there at Hugh Huffman's store."

We placed a grid of iron slats over the fire and then put a big tin pot on it for the coffee. After opening the cans of baked beans, we got spoons from one of the boxes and sat down on a log by the fire and began eating from the cans. The baked beans were cold and sticky but they smelled good and tasted so good that we ate them in a hurry and opened two more cans.

When the chicory coffee had boiled until it was black, we sat there in the firelight with the woodsmoke hovering around us and eating beans and drinking coffee and I was thinking I had never had a finer meal at home or anywhere else before. Smelling the mingled odor of smoke and coffee and listening to the sounds of the birds all around us so late in the night was like being in a strange part of the world thousands of miles away.

For a long time not a word was spoken. Then after a while Guthry said we had plenty of lard and cornmeal and that we would mix a batter the next morning and make hot cornmeal cakes in a frying pan to eat with fried bacon slabs for breakfast. But after that, he said with a wide smile, we were going to have fried catfish every time we sat down to eat.

We had finished eating the baked beans and were drinking more coffee when we heard Duke Hopkins call the first time from somewhere not far from the island. He sounded near enough not to be lost, but he did sound distressed about something.

3

WHEN WE GOT TO THE EDGE of the water where we had beached our skiff, Duke was calling louder than ever.

"Mister Guthry! Mister Guthry! Can't you hear me, Mister Guthry? You said you'd hear me!"

"Is that you, Duke?" Guthry answered him.

"It's me, Mister Guthry."

"What's the matter?"

"I'm in trouble."

"What trouble?"

"I'm rowing as hard as I can but I can't get an inch closer to that island."

"You remember how I told you to row that boat toward Chicago and Kansas City at the same time. Just keep your head and—"

"I don't want to go off to those places. I want to get where I can stand on solid ground in a hurry."

"Then all you have to do is keep that boat headed kitty-cornered like I told you."

"I'm doing that as hard as I can but it's still drifting down toward Memphis."

"All right, Duke. I'll tell you something else to do."

"What is that, Mister Guthry? Please hurry up and tell me!"

"Turn around and go back and get a good fast start next time. That current wasn't too strong for Steve and me to get across it a little while ago."

"Well, something must've speeded it up because it is now. And I don't want to go back near that mud flat at Little Dipper, either."

"What was all that shooting over there all about, Duke?" Guthry asked him.

"Could you hear it all the way over here?"

"I heard three shots."

66

"That's what I counted, too."

"What happened to Troy Pickett?"

"He's right here in the skiff with me now."

"Is he hurt? Did he get shot?"

"He didn't get shot, but he's still all winded and out of breath from running so hard."

"Did he get caught fooling around with that girl?"

"You ask him that yourself when he's ready to talk, Mister Guthry. Just tell me how to get to where you are. That's all I want to know now. I can see that fire burning behind you and I don't want to drift out of sight of it and get carried off down the river in this dark night."

"Then row for all you're worth and you'll get to some calm water pretty soon. If you drift some with the current, don't worry. All you have to do then is row back this way alongside the island. It won't be any trouble at all if you'll do like I tell you and don't lose your head and get flustered."

"I don't know where my head is now, but I know my hands are two big blisters."

In the dim starlight we could see the skiff gradually move forward and reach the calm water just before the current might have carried it out of sight at the lower end of the island. In a few minutes, Duke had rowed to where we were waiting and beached his skiff beside the other one. Troy climbed out, not saying a word, and stumbled up the bank toward the fire in the clearing.

While Troy and Duke were eating baked beans out of the cans, Guthry poured coffee into two tin cups for them. Troy still had not said anything until Guthry asked him what had caused the shooting at Little Dipper.

"I'm a sonofabitch," Troy said then. "I wasn't doing a goddam thing except standing there at my truck and whistling just a little bit. Then the first thing I knowed, that girl came out of the bushes and was right there in front of me close enough for me to reach out and touch. She didn't say a word while I was feeling her, and then when I grabbed her good, she still didn't say nothing or want to fight me off. But before I could get her down, Clyde Owens started shooting from somewhere in the bushes. I had to run like hell to get to the skiff and get away from there before he could shoot some more. Clyde Owens is a mean bastard."

"You could've been killed for that, Troy," Guthry told him, "and you know it."

"Maybe so, but next time I'll outsmart him before he can run me off. I ain't done yet."

"You'd better be done. And if you listen to me, you'll wait till you get back to Unionville where you know your way around."

"Hell, I can always get me a high-yellow back there. I save that for ordinary times. But a white girl goes good with a fishing trip and makes it real special. Anyhow, I was going to do her a favor—so she wouldn't get raped by a nigger. That's why I stayed there—to give her protection."

He pointed his finger at Duke.

"You heard me—you nigger bastard! You figured you was going to rape her, didn't you?"

68

Duke said nothing.

"Now, wait a minute, Troy," Guthry spoke up at once. "Just hold on here. There's no sense in talking like that. Be reasonable. You know why you went back to that truck and it wasn't because you'd forgotten something, either. And all that time Duke stayed at the boat landing waiting for you instead of rowing over here when Steve and I did and leaving you behind. Looks like you'd want to give him credit for that instead of accusing him of something he didn't do. If he hadn't waited for you, you'd have been in a hell of a fix. You could still be cornered over there by Clyde Owens to be shot at—and maybe even dead by now. And besides, we came down here to fish—not to quarrel. This island is big enough for four people to fish on but nowhere big enough for anybody to stay on and make trouble about nothing. Now, let's do what we came here for and nothing else."

Troy pointed at Duke again.

"Why don't he say something if he wasn't figuring on raping a white girl?"

"He doesn't have to say anything. Leave him alone, Troy, goddam it."

"I want to hear him lie about it."

"Mister Troy, please leave me out of it," Duke spoke up at last. "I didn't have anything to do with this and I didn't start this talk and I don't have anything to say about it."

"You don't have to say nothing—I know all about you niggers. I've been around them all my life and I know what they're thinking. I see them standing on the street

69

every day and looking white women up and down and thinking about them with no clothes on. Every goddam nigger man wants to rape a white woman. Let's hear you lie about that."

"You can say anything you please, Mister Troy, but I'm not talking."

"You'll talk if I tell you to!"

"But I won't lie."

Getting up from the log, Guthry walked around the campfire saying he did not think it would rain during the night and that it would be safe to wait until the next day to put up the sleeping tent. Duke unfolded the cots and spread a quilt over each one. Then he unrolled the bolt of mosquito netting and cut four pieces from it about the size of a sheet for us to put over us when we went to sleep. The mosquitoes were not bothering us then because the campfire made a good smudge to keep them away.

Troy got a bottle of bourbon from the gunnysack and poured a good amount of it into his tin coffee cup. After taking a drink of it, and nodding favorably, he handed the bottle to Guthry.

"It's time to have a drink," he stated with a friendly grin. "What the hell! Talk can wait but good red whiskey won't. I ain't mad at nobody now."

Guthry helped himself from the bottle and then poured some into Duke's cup. When he finished, he put the half-full bottle on the ground beside the log.

"You gave Duke some of that red whiskey," Troy said, "and why don't you give Steve a drink? Why do you treat a nigger better than a white boy?"

Guthry pointed at the bottle beside the log.

"Steve knows where the bottle is and if he wants a drink he'll get it himself. I'm not giving him a drink of whiskey and nobody else is, either. That's something for him to make up his own mind about at his age—not me or you. And don't you forget it, Troy. Steve came down here to learn on his own and that's the way it's going to be—just like finding out about gutting fish and cooking on a campfire. Or seeing you almost get shot to death by Clyde Owens."

"Hell, I'm not scared of Clyde Owens. I can go back over there when I want a woman and outsmart Clyde Owens twice a night in his own front yard."

FIVE

1

THE FIRST THING to be done after breakfast the next morning, Guthry said while all of us were sitting on the logs and eating around the campfire, was to hook and bait the trotline so we would have a good mess of catfish for the next meal instead of eating more baked beans.

The trotline was a strong, thin, tightly wound hemp rope we had brought with us and which was to be stretched for a distance of about fifty or sixty yards across the inside channel from a large flood-stranded hickory stump at the upper end of the island to the trunk of a dead cottonwood tree on the mainland near the mouth of Shady Creek.

About a dozen hooks were to be lead-weighted and tied to fishline trots about six feet long and then fastened to the trotline at ten-foot intervals where the lead-weighted trots would sink to the best depth to catch the largest catfish. Guthry had made strips of rags from a piece of white cloth to be tied to the top of each trot on the line. And then, too, the hemp rope had to be stretched taut enough to stay suspended above the water so that when a fish was caught we could see the line bob up and down and the strip of white cloth flutter like a flag and we would know exactly which hook it had taken.

When Guthry said it was time to bait the hooks with bacon rinds, which he wanted to do first of all and not after the trotline had been stretched across the narrows to Shady Creek, Troy Pickett immediately said that was the wrong way to do trotline fishing and that he wanted it done right or he would row back to Little Dipper and get in his truck and go home without us.

Troy had been quarrelsome and fault-finding and peevish ever since he got up that morning. To begin with, the noisy birds on the island woke him up when they began chirping again at daybreak and nobody else could sleep after he began yelling and swearing and throwing sticks at every bird he could see in the trees and bushes. Next, he had found fault with the coffee Duke made, saying it was too weak and puny for a white man like him to drink. And after that he had complained because we had no molasses to pour over the hot cornmeal cakes Guthry had cooked for breakfast.

The weather did not suit Troy, either. He said he could see a cloud coming up the river that looked like it would bring a steady all-day rain to ruin the fishing trip for him. Troy had done a lot of complaining and grumbling that morning but nobody said much to him until he began quarreling with Guthry about the best method of baiting the fishhooks for the trotline.

"You don't know a goddam nothing about trotline river fishing, Guthry Henderson," Troy said. "I've thrown back more fish than you ever saw on your hook."

"I've been around and caught a few fish in my time," Guthry told him.

"What kind of fish?" He stopped and laughed at Guthry. "I know what you mean. A lot of people like you think you're a goddam smart fisherman if you happen to luck-catch a puny trout or perch in a stinking cowpasture pond. Hell, that's old-woman fishing. I know more right now than you'll ever live to know about how to take catfish out of this goddam muddy river water."

"You can be right about everything you've said so far," Guthry told him. "I'm not going to argue about that. But, if we don't bait that trotline before we put it out there, somebody has to take a skiff and do it afterward. And it won't be easy to keep a skiff steady and bait all those hooks in that current. That's why it's better to do the baiting now and get it done at the start and save all that trouble."

"You put up the goddam trotline and I'll show you how to bait it like it ought to be done. Then you'll know more than you did before you came down here."

"Then tell me one thing."

"What's that?"

"Who's going to row the skiff and keep it steady for you in that swift current while you're baiting the hooks?"

"That's for Duke to do. He'll do what I tell him.

Ain't that one of the things he's doing here for? You told me he's an all-around nigger, didn't you? That's all there is to say. You go on and stretch the trotline. Then if you ain't too ashamed of yourself, you can watch me and you might learn a lot you don't know about fishing on this river. And then you can go back to town and boast all over about being a big trotline expert."

"All right, Troy," Guthry finally agreed with a wave of his hand. "I'm tired of arguing. Go ahead and do it your way. I didn't come all the way down here to quarrel. I came down here to catch fish and eat fish."

Guthry motioned to me.

"Come on, Steve. Let's stretch that rope over the channel the way it is and let Troy bait the trots the way he wants to afterward."

Guthry and I put the long hemp rope in a skiff and rowed to the upper end of the island. Even before we landed there we could see that the growth of trees and bushes and muscadine vines was like a jungle. In addition to the willows, which grew everywhere on Summertime Island, there were many other kinds of trees—oak, hickory, pine, maple, and locust—that had been washed downstream during the spring floods and had managed to take root and survive after snagging on stumps and other driftwood already there. Also, a few fruit trees had taken root—apple, peach, plum, and cherry—but were stunted and barely surviving under the shade of the tall willows.

After beaching the skiff at the point of the island, we

got out and stood there looking across the narrows. That was where the current was the strongest and we could see leaves and limbs and all kinds of driftwood swirling in the narrows on the way to the calm backwater.

The morning sun was already above the top of the cottonwood tree at Shady Creek and, about two hundred yards to the south of it at Little Dipper, we could see the dim glow of the sun on the rusty tin roof of Clyde Owens' house. We were too far away to be able to see Betty and her father anywhere around the house and boat landing.

"Just as I was saying before we left Unionville, you'll learn as much about people while we're down here as you will about fishing, Steve," Guthry told me as we stood there. He laughed a little to himself, evidently still thinking about the argument with Troy Pickett, and kicked at a piece of driftwood. "And the way it's started out, you'll learn a lot more than we'd counted on. And if we don't catch any fish, it'll still be worthwhile for you.

"Troy really had to have his own way about baiting the trotline, didn't he? Well, you have to come to a place like this on a camp-out to get true knowledge about both—people and fishing—something you might not be likely to learn as much about in schoolbooks in Unionville or Memphis."

Guthry turned over a piece of driftwood that looked like a newel from somebody's staircase.

"Steve, there're a lot of people in the world like Troy Pickett and you'll come across more and more of them

77

as you grow older. I get awfully provoked with Troy sometimes, but I can't get really mad at him no matter how he talks. I think I know how he feels and what causes it and I go out of my way to make allowances for the way he talks and acts. Since he has hardly no education himself, he resents anybody who's gone past the fourth or fifth grade—that's the stopping point in his life. And it could be the stopping point in his life even if he had gone to school a few years longer—instead of feeling inferior, he feels superior to anybody with normal or average education.

"And that is probably the reason why he becomes quarrelsome and contrary—just as he threatened to go away and leave us stranded down here if he couldn't have his way about baiting the trotline. And when it comes to a colored person like Duke Hopkins, who's educated enough to be a schoolteacher, I wouldn't put it past Troy to become so resentful that he'd think nothing of trying to harm Duke somehow because Duke is a Negro with a superior education.

"And Troy's not the only one—he's just one of thousands. There are a lot of white people like him in Unionville and everywhere else I've been in Tennessee and Kentucky. And from what I know about it, you'll find them down in Mississippi and Alabama, too. They're the white people who are cheating the colored out of a dollar in the store and short-weighing share-crop cotton or corn and voting down tax money for a colored school. And there won't be much of a change until a few generations of white people get out of the fifth-grade mentality and acquire more tolerance and humanity than they've got now. How's that for a Wednesday morning sermon before we've caught the first fish?

"But just remember that about Troy, Steve. If he tries to provoke you and pick a quarrel about something, just ignore it. Don't let it upset you. Just let him talk and get it out of his system. It gives him that feeling of superiority that he craves and nothing he says is going to hurt you. And you'll come out just a little bit wiser for having been exposed to it. Like I said about a camp-out—you'll learn firsthand something more than just spitting on a fishhook to bring good luck. Now, let's get the trotline up and catch those catfish. We're going to be good and hungry by the time the sun moves straight up overhead and it's racing up there right now."

2

We fastened one end of the line to the big stump and then trailed it behind us in the water while rowing across the narrows. The lead-weighted unbaited hooks had already been tied to the six-foot trots on the rope.

The channel current was just as swift as it had looked from the island and the skiff turned completely around several times in the swirling eddy before we reached the other side. After stretching the line as tightly as we could and tying it securely to the big cottonwood tree, we rowed back to the clearing on the island.

Troy was waiting for us and complaining about our not getting back sooner. He had cut the bacon rinds into bait-size chunks and had a bean can filled with them. As soon as Guthry and I landed on the bank, he and Duke got into the skiff and rowed to the trotline.

Troy began baiting at the island side of the line where there was very little current. Duke was able then to keep the skiff in a steady position while Troy leaned over the side to pull up a trot and bait the hook. All went well until they got to the middle of the channel where the current was strongest.

As we watched them, we could see that Duke was doing his best to keep the skiff steady while Troy was leaning over the side, but the swirling current was continually swerving the skiff back and forth and Troy was yelling at him and swearing about it. We knew how strong the current was and how difficult it would be for anybody to keep a flat-bottom boat in a steady position out there in the narrows for even a minute or two at a time.

There were three or four more fishhooks left on the trotline to bait when Troy, leaning too far over the side of the skiff, lost his balance and plunged headlong into the muddy water. That was when the skiff capsized, throwing Duke into the water also, and both the skiff and the two oars began drifting beyond reach with the current. We could see Duke swimming and keeping afloat while he looked for the nearest land, but Troy still had not come back to the surface.

While Guthry and I were getting into the other skiff to save the oars and get a tow on the overturned skiff before they were carried down the river in the current, we heard Troy yell for help. He had come to the surface for only a moment and then had disappeared again. As soon as we could take the floating oars aboard, and towing the capsized skiff, we began rowing as hard as we could to where we had last seen Troy.

We were rowing against the current and, before we could get very far, Duke had turned around and was swimming back to the narrows. We saw him dive into the water and disappear from sight. The longer Troy and Duke were under the water the more fearful we became that both of them had drowned.

It seemed as if minutes had passed before Duke at last came back to the surface. When he did come up, though, he had a grip on Troy's shirt and was keeping Troy's head above water. Guthry and I were still far away and the swift current was keeping us almost at a standstill. However, not waiting for us, Duke began swimming to the island with an arm around Troy's neck while keeping his head above water.

When we got to the bank, Duke had stretched Troy face down on the ground and was working on him to pump the water out of his lungs and trying to bring back his breathing.

"Jesus Christ!" Guthry said, getting down on his knees beside Troy. "He was a dead man out there in that water. Coffin-dead. He'd still be a dead man if you hadn't got him out of there as quick as you did, Duke. Do you think he's going to be all right now?"

"He's coming around. He's breathing better now. I guess we got him out in time."

"Well, if he comes out of this, he'd better learn how to swim before he ever comes back down here again and tips over a boat. How in the world did you ever find him down there in that muddy water? You couldn't see anything, could you?"

"I couldn't see but I could feel. I went right down on the bottom and caught up with him before the current carried him off."

Troy, moaning weakly, turned on his side. Then when he opened his eyes, he looked up and recognized Duke bending over him.

"What the hell you doing?" he said weakly, still breathing slowly. "I don't allow no dinges close to me. Get away from here."

"Goddam it, Troy! Shut up!" Guthry shouted at him.

Duke stood up then and began walking into the clearing.

"You're a damn fool, Troy," Guthry told him. "Don't you know Duke Hopkins saved your life? You're lucky to be alive and breathing—and Duke did it. I couldn't do anything out there in time to help you—I was too far away. You'd still be out there on the bottom of that water if it hadn't been for Duke—or else dead and gone twenty miles down the river by now. He went down and found you and brought you here. You'd better think about that some."

"It was his fault. He wasn't keeping the boat steady for me like I told him to."

"And you couldn't have kept it steady yourself, either. Nobody could. I was out there in that swift current—and I know about it. You can't keep on blaming him. Now shut up about that."

Moving his body weakly, Troy sat up for the first time since Duke had dragged him up the bank. His shirt and pants were dripping wet and he tried to squeeze out some of the muddy water. Then he took off his shoes and socks so they would dry more quickly. His face was pale and his breathing was in short gasps.

Saying nothing more to Troy then, Guthry stood up to look at the trotline. Several of the hooks were pulling on it and making it bob up and down.

"Come on, Duke," he called into the clearing. "We've got catfish hooked out there. Let's go get them."

"I'm coming, Mister Guthry," he said as he walked toward us. "But be careful. I don't want to go out there and get tipped over again. I've had enough of that for one day."

"Listen to him brag about what he done," Troy said. "What'd I tell you about him acting stuck-up with a name like he's got and being a schoolteacher?"

3

AFTER GUTHRY AND DUKE had shoved the skiff into the water and were rowing to the trotline, Troy watched them in silence until Guthry pulled up the first catfish and put new bait on the hook. That was when Troy asked me if I had seen Duke dive under water for him and bring him to land.

"Is that the real truth, Steve?" he asked after I had told him what exactly had happened. "Did he really do it all by himself? You and Guthry didn't help none at all? Don't you lie to me about a nigger."

I told him that Guthry and I were too far away, and rowing against the current, too, to get there in time to help Duke.

"I'm a sonofabitch," he said slowly, shaking his head as he looked across the backwater at Guthry and Duke.

He appeared to be fully recovered by then although his face was still pale and he did not try to get to his feet. Now and then, displeased and unhappy because Duke alone had saved his life, he continued to shake his head.

"I never thought I'd ever have to be thankful to a black bastard of a nigger for doing something like that for me. But don't you tell him I said so. It makes me mad as hell to know that. But that ain't going to keep me from hating every goddam one of them that's ever been born. Because I'll always hate niggers—and be glad of it."

He turned to me with a hopeful expression.

"Tell me God's own truth, Steve. You don't like them neither, do you?"

I told him that I had no reason to dislike them just because their color was not the same as mine.

He scooped up a handful of dirt and threw it as far as he could over the backwater.

"You talk just like your uncle. What kind of white people are you Hendersons, anyhow?"

All I could think of saying was to tell him once more that I had no reason to dislike Negroes.

"Maybe there's a little bit of excuse for you," he said

with a slight smile. "You come from Memphis. City people down there in Memphis don't know about niggers
like I do. But you'd better by God hurry up and learn
if you're going to keep on living where the niggers grow
like pig weeds. If you don't learn about them, they'll
find out about you and start stepping on your toes on
purpose and doing everything else they want to around
white people. Hell, they'll think they can take over the
whole country if they're not kept in their place and
beat down. Some of them like Duke Hopkins think
that way now—I know what niggers think in their heads.
You pay attention to me. I'll learn you about them.

"I've been like I am all my life and won't nothing
never change me—not even what Duke Hopkins done.
And he only done that so he could boast about it. When
I was a kid five or six years old and played with them—
and that was before I knowed better than to play
with niggers—I used to come up behind one of the little
niggers when he wasn't looking and hit him as hard as
I could with my fist every chance I got. And I'd hit
one of them with a bottle or a rock when I could. And
drive a rusty nail in a board and hide it under some
grass so they'd step on it barefooted. If they got a rusty
nail rammed up their foot, that's what I liked best. Because that's when they'd yell for their mammy like all
hell broke loose.

"Now you know how I learned right from the start
how to treat niggers. I don't go around driving rusty
nails in boards for them to step on no more. I've got
something better to do now. I like to try to run down
a nigger with my truck when I can catch him crossing

the street before he sees me in time to jump out of the way. I sure do like to see the blacks jump like that—it keeps them from forgetting about white people being around. And they can't do a goddam thing about it, neither. White people ain't going to testify against me— and the blacks are scared to. Right now in Unionville most niggers know me when they see me coming in my truck and they'll start running like hell when I'm still a block away.

"But I'll tell you something else about me. I'm a fool about high-yellow gals. Goddam right I am. I like them when they're about twelve or fourteen years old—that's the best time—and I mean the real light colored that don't even have kinky hair and look like they could almost pass for white if they tried. That's the best high-yellow kind, believe me, and nobody knows more about it than me. If you ain't done it yet, you try it and see if I didn't tell you God's own truth. Of course, it's liable to spoil you for all the rest of your life for ordinary white girls, like it did me, but you'll be glad you done it. The good thing about it is because they can be real goody and bouncy right from the start and not all stiff and stubborn like most white girls.

"I like to talk about that. And it'll do a young boy like you just starting out a lot of good to know about it. I started out with high-yellow gals when I was about twelve or thirteen and I've kept it up ever since. And I wouldn't want them much older now than I ever did— maybe around fifteen now—and I know so much about it now I know how to get one whenever I want to. And after the first few of them, you learn how not to waste time about it.

"I'm riding around town in my truck all day hauling freight and express from the depot and I keep my eyes open. Then when I see one that looks good to me, I stake out the ground and then go back right after sundown. That's the best time of all. It's just about halfway dark enough then for no buck nigger or old woman to see what's going on and bother you. The high-yellow I'm looking for will be coming out of a house or a store and going through a vacant lot or someplace like that where I can head her off. All I have to do then is scare the hell out of her to make her stay quiet and not start yelling when I throw her down. You try that and see if it don't work out just like I say. And you can take my word for it. After you've done it once, you'll see how easy it is and won't never be backward about it no more from then on."

Troy stopped talking while he looked across the water at Guthry and Duke in the skiff. They had almost reached the end of the trotline at Shady Creek by then and would soon be rowing back to the island with the catch of fish.

"But that don't make me like the buck niggers," Troy said presently. "And Duke Hopkins is right at the top of the list now. I've sure got it in mean for him from now on. He'll be swell-headed now more than ever for getting me out of that water. What else makes me so goddam mad is he was already stuck-up to start with. I can get along with niggers as long as they behave like niggers ought to around white people. But he acts like he thinks it makes him better than me because he's a schoolteacher and has got all those books he reads.

"Hell, I can read and write my own name—and I'm white and he ain't and won't never be. It's that name of his that made him stuck-up before he left town and came down here. Duke! There's never been a real duke who was a nigger bastard—people wouldn't allow that. He ought to be run out of the country if he don't change his name. If he's left alone like it is, the next thing the nigger bastard will do is pick out a white woman to rape. I can read his mind about that. That's what he's after. And after he'd done it, he'd be so biggety about it he'll claim she wanted him to do it and begged him. That's why he needs putting in his place and beat down before he can do that. If it'd been him who fell out of that skiff a while ago and couldn't swim, he'd be down there on the bottom of that backwater right now—or else going down the river somewhere like a stick of driftwood. But getting drowned out there would be too good for him—unless he had his balls cut off first. And don't think that ain't been done, too. I know because I've been there to help do it to buck niggers like him."

Guthry and Duke came back from the trotline with a catch of several big catfish and began cleaning them right away for frying. It was noon then and the storm cloud we had seen far down the river that morning was moving closer and the sun was barely visible in the overcast sky. Guthry said that while the catfish were cooking we should hurry and put up the sleeping tent so we would have a place to keep dry when the rain came. There was a strong wind blowing up the river, too, and some of the birds that lived on the island had come back from the mainland and were chirping and fluttering in the dense bushes as if they expected rain any minute and were taking cover.

While Guthry, Duke, and I were raising the tent and staking the guys, Troy got a bottle of bourbon from the gunnysack and sat down on one of the cots with a tin cup. He had taken several drinks by the time we had finished putting up the tent and was feeling good enough to shout at the noisy birds and throw sticks at them. It had been about two hours since he was brought out of the water and, except for a slight paleness of his face, he appeared to be his usual self again.

"Hey, Guthry!" he called out in a loud voice. "Come over here!"

Guthry finished turning over the fish in the frying pan before going to the cot.

"Do you want to know what I'm going to do?" Troy asked him.

"What?"

He handed the bottle to Guthry.

"Take a drink first and then I'll tell you."

Guthry poured some bourbon into a cup.

"Are you thinking about going out there again to bait the trotline, Troy?"

"Hell, no. That's for you and the nigger to do. I'm going to get a bellyful of fried catfish and red whiskey and then take a nap. That's the first thing. Then after that rain comes and goes, I'm going to get in a skiff and row over to that boat landing at Clyde Owens' place about sundown."

"What for, Troy?"

"Don't look so worried, Guthry. I'm not going to drive off and leave you down here. I'm going over there to clean the spark plugs in my truck engine. They're all fouled up and need cleaning bad before we start back to Unionville."

"Why don't you wait till it's daylight tomorrow so you can see what you're doing?"

"I can feel my way around in the dark."

Guthry nodded and then took another drink from his tin cup.

"Well, Troy, there's just one thing I want you to do before you go over there tonight."

"What's that?"

"Tell me if you want to be buried over there on the spot or if we'll have to haul your dead body all the way back to the cemetery in Unionville."

SIX

1

THERE HAD BEEN a good full catch on the trots during the night—including a buffalo and a carp, both of which we threw back—and Duke and I went to work cleaning eight big catfish for the next meal as soon as we finished eating breakfast that morning. For several hours between midnight and dawn there had been a drizzly rainfall and Guthry said that made the best kind of fishing weather anybody could hope for and was the reason why we had such a good catch.

The day had started out being clear and sunny, however, with only a few puffy white clouds far up the river. It was already calm and balmy early in the morning, too, and we knew it would be a good day for swimming. Duke and I had already found that the best place for swimming was off the bank in the main channel where the river was much more clear and fresh than the backwater.

In the beginning, Duke and I had been talking about a red-stack towboat we saw towing two barges up the river earlier that morning. Then later, for some reason, we began talking about girls and why some of them were so particular about keeping their legs covered above their knees and why others would sometimes pull up their dresses almost to their hips to show off their legs. Finally, Duke said girls were such a mystery that the best thing for us to do was study them one at a time.

After we had cleaned about half the catch, Duke reached into the tin fish tub we were using and picked up the largest catfish by the gills. Holding it up in front of us, he looked at it admiringly with a wide smile. We did not have a scale to weigh the big fish, but Duke said it was the largest catfish he had ever seen and might be the biggest in the whole Mississippi River. All the other fish in the catch were much smaller and most of them were about half that size.

"Steve, just look at that bossy old man," Duke said, still smiling with admiration. "Just look at that bossy face with those long tomcat whiskers sticking out at us. He'd win the first prize in any catfish show. Just look at him in the face! He'd scare anybody out of his way if you met him face-to-face down under the water somewhere. I bet he was the big boss of the whole Mississippi River between Memphis and St. Louis. And everywhere else he went, too. Up the big creeks and little rivers. Trailing the steamboats and nosing along the levees. Chasing all the other fish away so he could get the best bite of something to eat. He could go anywhere he pleased when he had a notion and didn't have to ask anybody if he could or couldn't.

"That's the way to live. It's something a lot of people can't do—and I'm one of them. I sure envy him and wish I could go where I wanted to like that bossy old man. All the way down the big river to New Orleans and then turn around and come back up this way. And all the time all he needed was enough water to swim in. There's no telling where all he'd go up the river from here—maybe all the way to the beginning of it. And not just once, either. He could do that anytime he felt like it. But one thing he oughtn't have done was leave the main channel and come over here to this back-water slough and get hooked in the narrows."

Duke put the big fish back into the tub and went to the sleeping tent where he kept his tackle box. When he came back, he was carrying his geography textbook and had opened it to one of the large double-page maps. He put his finger on the map to point to the place where he thought we were then.

"This island's not much bigger than an ordinary sand bar and too little to show on the map, but it ought to be right about here. Someday I'd like to see some maps big enough to show everything in the whole country. Then I'd like to start out and travel around and see all there is from beginning to end. Just look at all the long rivers and big cities everywhere. And I bet there're plenty of little creeks and small towns everywhere, too."

After studying the map for a while, he took a deep breath, and then he looked at me.

"Steve, tell me something," he said. "How far away from home have you ever been in your life? Have you ever been all the way down to New Orleans or up to St. Louis and places like that?"

I told him that I had been in Arkansas and Mississippi and to other parts of Tennessee but nowhere else.

"That's just like me, Steve," he said, shaking his head and bending over the map again. "I've never been far away, either. Only in Kentucky and right here in this part of Tennessee. And just look at how much more there is in this great big country between the two blue oceans. All the rivers and mountains and towns scattered all over. I bet that old man catfish has been to a lot more places than both of us put together. I don't know what he saw, except other catfish, but he was getting around like I want to do. I don't want to stay in one place all my life like an old hickory stump in the ground. After I've been around plenty, I might settle down somewhere and be satisfied. But not now. I'm sure about that. It's too early in my life for that when there's so much to see."

We sat there and looked at the large map showing all the states in various colors and the rivers in heavy blue lines and big black circles where the cities were located. Presently Duke began tracing with his finger the blue lines of the Ohio River and the Missouri River and others that looked like the bare limbs and branches of a giant tree after shedding all its leaves in winter.

"That old man catfish got me all stirred up and made my feet feel limber and ready to go," he said after a while, looking across the backwater toward Little Dipper Landing. "And now I've made up my mind about it for sure. One of these days I'm going to start out and travel around this big country. And I don't want anybody to stop me and tell me I can't go where I please. That would be the worst thing to happen to me."

He paused, remaining silent for several moments as if something else of importance had come to mind.

"But I'll have to hurry," he said then, "and get started before a frisky gal comes along and makes herself free and easy and gets me married to her. That'd be an awful thing to happen to me before I could get going. I know all about it, because I've already had some trying to do just that to me and it gets harder every time to keep away from them. They're smart people about that. When they get all soft and loving and down to naked—look out! They're born knowing how to do that and being frisky and that means—look out, boy! But I know something, too. You couldn't travel far enough and fast enough and get to all the places once you're married—that's when you have to settle down and stay in one place and work at a steady job. That's why I'm going to hold off from getting married for a while longer—if I can."

Duke laughed to himself about that for a moment, and then suddenly he was shaking his head.

"The only trouble is that right now I'm staying single but still can't go off everywhere like that big old catfish could—and like white people do. That's what makes all the difference in the world. Being my color. A colored fellow like me has to watch his step all the time and stay mighty close to where the other colored live. That's the big bad thing about being colored—black, brown, or tan. I know all about it, because the white policemen have told me to keep off the streets where the white people live and don't even go near their stores unless I've got money in my pocket to buy something and then to hurry off again and don't hang around and go back where I belong.

"I know a lot about that kind of talk. I went to Louisville once—just a few years ago—and I was walking along the street after dark one night looking at the sights where the big stores are and a policeman came up behind me and rapped me real hard on the back of my neck with his billy club and told me to get going and hurry back where the colored lived. I told him I came from Paducah and didn't live in Louisville and was just looking at the big-city sights. He said that made no difference to him because a nigger is a nigger no matter where he comes from. I've heard a lot of that in my time—a nigger is a nigger.

"The same thing happened to me in Unionville not long ago. It was just like it was in Louisville up in Kentucky. This time the white policeman didn't say the exact same thing. But I could tell what he had in his mind about it. A nigger is a nigger no matter what. Anyhow, I'd gone downtown in Unionville and was looking at the lighted store windows around the courthouse square after dark and the night policeman came up and poked me real hard in the ribs with his billy club and told me to go back to Prospect Avenue or somewhere else in the Negro quarter.

"That hard poke in the ribs with the billy club really

hurt, but I didn't complain about it. I just told him that I only wanted to walk around the square and look at the store windows and nothing else. Saying only that made him mad and he told me to tell him if I had a job and who I worked for. I told him I was the geography and history teacher in the colored school and had a little barbershop of my own where I worked on Saturdays. When I told him that, he said I was boasting about being educated and arguing with him instead of doing what he told me and that he'd put me in the lock-up and keep me there a week if I didn't get out of sight by the time he counted nine. I don't know why he'd only count to nine instead of to ten unless he figured that would make me run faster. And sure enough, he started counting—one—two—three—and there wasn't a thing I could do then except run like hell to stay out of jail. He was like a lot of them—they like to make a colored man run. It gives some white people a good feeling to order a colored fellow around like that.

"When they talk to me that way, that's the only time I wish I could be white and talk back to them as sassy as I pleased. It's not that I feel mean about it—I just want to say what I think.

"But what bothers me the most is that it's likely to keep on being the same—like it was in Louisville and Unionville—no matter where I go. I've heard colored people who've been to Cincinnati and Chicago and other big cities say it's not much different everywhere else. Maybe someday somehow times will change better for the colored. But what I'm afraid of is that they won't change soon enough to help me at all before I'm dead and gone. Right now it stays the same. One—two—three—a nigger is a nigger—and get the hell back to Prospect Avenue or wherever the Negro quarter is. One—two—three—"

2

THERE WERE STILL more fish in the tub to be cleaned for cooking when we heard Troy Pickett calling Duke.

"Where's that nigger boy?" Troy shouted.

Duke muttered to himself. "One—two—three—"

We were about fifty feet from the middle of the clearing and Guthry was on the other side of the island fishing in the main channel of the river with a pole and line.

Duke turned around and looked behind him. We could see Troy tramping in a circle at the campfire.

"Boy!" Troy yelled more loudly than he had the first time. "You'd better hear me! You know what you're down here for! Come here and fix me something to eat and hurry up about it!"

Troy had come back to the island from Little Dipper Landing in the middle of the night and woke up everybody with his loud swearing while he was trying to find his cot in the dark. While Troy was still sleeping late that morning, Guthry had said he had not heard any pistol shots in the night and that it was his guess that Clyde Owens had had the good sense to lock up his daughter in the house and that Troy had to spend the time cleaning spark plugs after all. He said if that was what had happened, he expected Troy to be meaner than ever that day.

"I see you!" Troy called out. "You can't hide from me! Hurry up! You're down here to do what you're told! You hear me, boy!"

"I hear you, Mister Troy," Duke said calmly. "Steve and I are cleaning fish now and we want to get it finished before anything else. It'll take a little while longer and then I'll be there."

Troy came walking slowly toward us. He picked up a piece of driftwood and slashed at some of the overhanging willow branches.

"I'm a sonofabitch!" he said when he stopped a few yards away. "Niggers do what a white man tells them! What kind of a nigger do you think you are? Don't you know all niggers have to be the same? You're so goddam stuck-up you act like you think you're too good to do what I tell you! I'll show you! I'm going to beat hell out of you!"

Duke put the fish he was cleaning back into the tub and walked toward Troy.

"I don't want to get in a scrap with you, Mister Troy," he said. "But if you hit me—I can't help myself—I'll have to hit back."

"You goddam nigger bastard! You hit me just once and it'll be the last time you're alive to hit a white man! Goddam you! I'll kill you!"

"Mister Troy, I'd rather talk about it than get in a scrap over it."

"Shut up! You don't tell me what you want to do!"

99

Guthry, who had been fishing for the past hour from the bank on the other side of the island, came walking hurriedly into the clearing. He was carrying his fishing pole and bait can and had one small catfish not much larger than a fingerling.

"That's enough of that," Guthry called out. "Everybody calm down. I heard all this fussing and we don't want to have this kind of trouble. We didn't come down here for that."

"You stay out of this, Guthry Henderson," Troy told him angrily. "I'm taking care of this and I know what I'm going to do and nobody's going to stop me. I'm going to beat hell out of that nigger. He's been begging for it and now he's going to get it. The stuck-up goddam nigger bastard! Now stay out of my way, Guthry."

"What did he do, Troy?"

"It ain't what he done—it's what he ain't done. He wouldn't come and fix me something to eat when I told him to. He said he was too busy doing something else. Any nigger ought to know better than that and sense enough to step lively when I say so."

"That's nothing to fight about, Troy. Calm down. Let him finish cleaning fish. Go fix yourself something to eat. Anybody can do that."

"Hell, no! I ain't going to do it! That's what he's down here for—to jump and do what he's told like a good nigger does!"

Crouching forward, and with both fists ready, Troy moved closer to Duke.

Duke moved backward several steps.

"You nigger bastard!" Troy yelled at him. "Goddam your black liver!"

"Nasty name-calling won't settle a thing, Mister Troy," Duke said, taking another step backward, "and if I have to hit back at you, it'll make everything worse. Don't make me fight you. I've never been in a scrap with a white man before and I don't want to be in one now. But if—"

"You hit me just once! I dare you!"

"But I don't want to."

"Go ahead and do it."

Duke shook his head. "I'm not going to hit you first. You'll have to hit me first."

"And I'll do it, too. Then I'll stomp your nigger head out of sight in the ground. They won't have to dig a hole to bury you in—you'll already be buried."

Guthry tried to get between them, but Troy shoved him out of the way.

"Call if off, Troy," Guthry begged him, pulling at his arm. "Call it off!"

"Keep out of my way! I'm going to get him!"

"I'm warning you, Troy. You'd better listen to me. Duke's strong enough to hurt you."

"I ain't scared of no nigger!"

"All right. But I'm not going to try to stop him if he gets you down."

"I don't need no help!"

"Then whatever happens—don't blame me."

With a running leap, Troy kicked Duke as hard as he could in the crotch of the legs. Staggering backward from the unexpected blow, Duke dropped to his knees but did not fall to the ground. It was such a painful blow that the muscles of his neck tightened and throbbed and his lips were quivering.

While Duke was kneeling on the ground, still not fully recovered, Troy tried to kick him again. This time Duke grabbed his foot and threw him down on his back with a jarring thud.

Before Troy was able to move, Duke clamped his arm around Troy's neck with a strangling hold. After that, each time Troy struggled to free himself, Duke tightened his grip a little more and Troy finally lay there on the ground with a harmless kicking of his feet. He was able to breathe enough but he was choked so tightly by Duke's arm that he could barely whisper when he tried to talk.

We could hear Troy's faint whisper. "I'll get you yet. Goddam you. I'm going to kill you. You won't never do this to another white man."

Duke tightened his arm around Troy's neck.

"Be careful what you do, Duke," Guthry said to him, concerned. "Don't choke him too much. That's a dangerous hold you've got on him. Be sure to let him have enough air to keep breathing."

Duke looked up and nodded. "I'll watch that," he said. "But I'm not going to turn him loose till he's ready to quit and say he'll quit."

"It won't be like Troy to give up to you—unless you've got him so he can't help himself."

"I don't know what he's going to do about it but I

know what I'm going to do. I'm not going to let him get up and kick me like that again. I'm going to watch out for myself."

3

GUTHRY GOT DOWN on his knees beside them.

"Troy, listen to me. Duke's got you down on the ground and you can't do anything about it. You started this fight and I'm not going to make him break his hold. Are you ready to quit and say you'll leave him alone now?"

Troy managed to shake his head slightly.

"Hell, no," he said in a feeble whisper.

"Listen to me, Troy. We didn't come all the way down here to have this kind of trouble and there's no good reason for it. You ought to know that as well as I do. Duke got his hold on you fair-and-square. Now you've got to give up to get out of it. I'll be here, and I won't let him choke you to death, but that's all I'm going to do about it. I don't care if he is colored and you're white. This's different. He's got a right to keep you from hurting him. Why don't you tell Duke you'll leave him alone from now on and get this over with?"

Troy moved his head slightly.

"I ain't going to," he said weakly. "Goddam you, Guthry Henderson. You're taking up for him. I'll get even with both of you."

Duke immediately tightened the headlock once more. Troy's face had been flushed until then, but, with the tightening of Duke's arm around his neck and throat, his face became pale and bloodless and there was not even a feeble twitching of his feet after that. He was beginning to look as lifeless as he was when Duke brought him out of the water the day before.

"What's he going to do about it, Mister Guthry?" Duke asked.

"I don't know," Guthry told him. "I've never seen anybody before as stubborn as he is. But watch what you're doing—don't choke the life out of him. That stranglehold can kill anybody."

"I'll watch out for that—and I'm watching out for myself, too. I'm not going to let him get up and kick me again. He'd try to kill me. He said so."

Guthry got up from his knees and stood there looking down at Troy.

"When I was a kid, I used to wrestle with little colored boys myself, but I've never seen a colored man and a grown-up white man get in a tussle like this before. As I know it, a colored man will always back away and run off before he'll get in this kind of scrap with a white man. I've seen shooting and knifing, but nothing like this."

"Maybe so, Mister Guthry," Duke said. "But I'm not running off. Not me. I'll stay right here all day and all night with my hold on him like this if I have to. If he wants to leave me alone, all he has to do is say so. That's all there is to it. And I'm not joking. I'm not going to let him kick me around just because I'm colored and he's white. He's got more rights than I have, but that doesn't mean I don't have any at all."

Troy could hear what was being said. With a weak blinking of his eyes, he shook his head as much as he could from time to time.

"Look here, Duke," Guthry said. "If he'll say he won't kick you again and try to fight more, will you turn him loose?"

"How will I know he won't be lying if he says it?"

"You could give him a chance to tell the truth."

"But just suppose it won't be the truth."

"You can get another headlock on him."

"I don't want to scrap him again."

"Somebody has to quit first."

"Let him do the quitting. He started it."

"You can see how he's acting. He's stubborn about it. He's too proud to give up to a colored man."

"I can't help that, Mister Guthry. All I know is that I've got a good wrestling hold on him now and that ought to be the end of it. In a wrestling match, there has to be a winner and a loser or it won't decide a thing. If he'll say I'm the winner—and one other thing, too—I'll let him loose right away. But you and Steve will have to be the witnesses to prove he said it if he goes back on his word and claims he didn't make the promise."

"What is this other thing you want him to agree to— aside from saying you're the winner?"

"I'll say it if he's ready to listen to me."

"Did you hear that, Troy?"

Duke loosened the headlock enough so that Troy would be able to talk.

Troy slowly blinked his eyes and we could see him staring blankly at us. He should have been able to hear what was being said, but either he was too weak to say anything or he was ready to agree to anything by that time. It seemed as if it had been at least half an hour since Duke grabbed his foot and threw him on the ground.

"You'd better listen to this, Troy," Guthry told him. "Now, Duke, what is this other thing you want him to promise?"

Duke looked down at Troy's pale face.

"It won't do any good to say it yet unless he's going to listen."

"Did you hear that, Troy?" Guthry asked.

Troy nodded weakly.

"All right, Duke," Guthry told him. "Go ahead and say it. What is it?"

Duke glanced at Troy's face for a moment.

"Well, if he had wrestled me down and I had to give up, I'd have to do what he said, wouldn't I? Isn't that the way it would be, Mister Guthry?"

"I suppose so."

"Then I don't want to have to jump and do everything he tells me to after this just because I'm colored and he's white—I'll do my share, and more, too—and I don't want to have to call him Mister Troy, either, after the way he kicked me. I want to call him just plain

Troy. Just like I'm plain Duke. That's the fair thing to do after the way he treated me."

"I'll get in on that myself," Guthry spoke up at once. "I'm all for it. I don't have to be called Mister Guthry— just like I don't want Steve to call me Uncle Guthry. It doesn't seem the right way to live when we've all been cramped close together like this on this little sand bar of an island—eating together and sleeping in the same tent and things like that. I bet there wouldn't have been any of this scrapping and fighting if we'd all started out doing that in the beginning. A camp-out fishing trip down here ought to be equal living for everybody—white and colored—and nobody ordered around and made to say Mister Guthry and Mister Troy. And somehow Summertime Island seems like the right place for equal living."

Guthry got down on the ground beside Troy.

"That's the way it's going to be, Troy. I know you heard all that. Are you ready to go along with it now?"

He made no reply.

"All right, Duke," Guthry said then. "Let him loose. That's enough."

"But how can I be sure he's going to give up and won't try to kick me again?"

"He's ready to quit—I can tell."

Duke moved away and got to his feet. As he stood there cautiously watching Troy, he began brushing the dirt from his clothes.

With a weak moan, and a slight twitching of his feet, Troy turned over and lay prone on the muddy earth.

"Come on, Steve," Guthry said with a motion of his hand. "Let's get him off that wet ground and carry him to a cot."

With Duke helping, we took him to the sleeping tent and put him on his cot and covered him with a quilt.

"Is he—is Troy—not going to bother me now when I call him Troy?" Duke asked with a look of uncertainty.

"He won't be bothering you, Duke." Guthry smiled then. "Guthry says so."

SEVEN

1

IN THE MIDDLE of the afternoon, the hottest part of the day when even the air itself felt sticky and sweaty, Duke and I stripped off our clothes and jumped into the river at the upper end of the island where the water was not too deep. As usual at that time of year, the water in the main channel of the river was slightly muddy. However, the run-off from the spring floods upstream had already carried most of the mud and trash downstream or into a backwater slough.

The weather that afternoon was still sunny and balmy and Duke said he was sure the temperature was at least ninety degrees and that it might even be closer to a hundred degrees. There were no clouds within sight to bring a thunderstorm to cool the air before nightfall.

Not far from where we went swimming, but out of sight behind the dense growth of drooping willows, Guthry was fishing again in the main channel with a long pole and bacon-rind bait. Troy had been up once to get himself something to eat and then he had gone back to his cot in the sleeping tent to take another nap.

Guthry had said we were not close enough to bother his fishing because all he really cared about was to be able to sit there in the shade of the willow trees where everything was quiet and peaceful and that it made no difference whether he caught anything or not because we could always take catfish off the trotline when we wanted something to eat. He had already been sitting on the riverbank and dozing most of the time for an hour or longer before Duke and I got there and he still had not caught a single fish.

Duke and I had started out splashing in the water with running jumps and belly-flops from the bank and later we began diving under water to find out what we could feel with our hands on the river bottom. Since the water was slightly muddy—and there was a thunderstorm somewhere upstream nearly everyday in summer that washed red or yellow clay into the river—we could not see the bottom no matter how shallow the water was. The only thing we found on the river bottom were a few sticks of waterlogged driftwood.

We had been there for about half an hour when we happened to glance around and saw three strangers standing on the bank watching us. We were so surprised to see anybody else on the island that for a moment we just stood there and stared at them.

Two of the strangers were tall burly looking men dressed in the kind of old clothes and droopy field-straw hats that most men wore when they came down to the river to fish. They took off their hats to fan their faces in the heat, and we could see that one of the men had heavy eyebrows and bushy black hair and the other one had thin yellowish hair and was partly bald-headed. Both men looked to be about thirty-five years old.

The other stranger was a slender girl not more than nineteen or twenty years old who was wearing a pink cotton dress and had thick dark-brown hair that was long enough to reach to her shoulders. She was pretty and bare-legged and had breasts that pushed against her tight pink dress and were moving slightly all the time.

The two men remained glum and stern-faced, but the girl was smiling at us.

When Duke and I had first seen the three strangers, we were standing on the bottom and, since we were naked, we had soon crouched down even lower after that until only our heads and shoulders were above water. None of them had spoken to us until one of the men asked how much longer we were going to camp on the island. He had a booming loud voice and he talked in a gruff manner as if he would tell us that we had no right to be there and would order us to go away.

I told him that I was not sure about when we would be leaving and that he ought to go toward the lower end of the island and ask Guthry about that.

Saying nothing more, the two men started walking along the bank to where Guthry was fishing and Duke and I waited for the girl to go with them so we could get out of the river and put on our clothes.

However, the girl stayed where she was and stood

there watching us. She was still smiling but did not say anything. We were waiting for her to leave when she took off her shoes, and then unfastened her dress and took that off, too. While I was watching her, I could hear Duke mutter to himself over and over again.

After hanging the pink dress on a bush, the girl began wading straight to where we were in the water. She had not taken off her underclothes, but they were much more skimpy than a bathing suit would have been and only partly covered her bouncy breasts. When she got to where we were crouching down, she was still only waist-deep in the water and, when she splashed herself, her thin underclothes became so skin-tight that she looked almost completely undressed. Crawling on his knees, Duke moved behind me. He was talking to himself again.

Smiling and friendly, the girl came so close that I could have reached out and touched her. There were a few freckles on her shoulders and a small brown spot above one of her breasts.

The first thing she said was that she wanted to know what our names were.

I told her that my name was Steve Henderson and that Duke's full name was Duke Hopkins.

"My name is Bonnie," she said, moving even closer. "Where did you come from?"

I told her that we came from Unionville.

Pouting and twisting her shoulders, she shook her head disdainfully.

"That place! I've been to Unionville. It's a so-so town. I never had a good time there. It's too dead for me. I live about fifteen miles from Unionville—Paxton. Paxton, Tennessee. You put both towns together and you still wouldn't have anything. I really come from another place about ten miles from Paxton. I ran away from home two years ago—I didn't like the way my stepmother tried to boss me around all the time. She said I was too sweet on men and handed out too much sugar. About the only thing in Paxton—Paxton, Tennessee—is a big sawmill and cross-tie plant—and the café where I work. The Crystal Palace—and what a garbage dump! But I won't be a waitress there much longer—I've got other plans. St. Louis, I hope. I've never been there but I hear it's a real good-time place. That's what I need.

"You saw those two friends of mine just now—they're Bubba Youngblood and Billy Roy Smith. Bubba's the one with a lot of real black hair—and looks like he never gets a haircut. And if Billy Roy got a haircut there wouldn't be enough to fill a thimble. They are cross-tie contractors for the railroad and they come in the café nearly every day and I've been dating both of them. Well, one at a time—I'm a nice girl. But you know what I mean—the kind of dates men want when they want it. Early dates—late dates—in-between dates. Anyway, they wanted me to come down here with them while they fished for a few days—to keep them company. They're married men and their wives don't know a thing about it—I mean, about me and coming down here. I don't care if they're married. I just want to have a good time. I'm always looking for a good time. Don't you like to have a good time, Steve?"

While I was nodding, Bonnie was looking at Duke.

She splashed more water on herself but was careful not to get her hair wet.

"I bet he's an Indian boy," she said then, smiling at Duke. "That's what he is."

Duke opened his mouth as if he wanted to say something, but all he could do was shake his head.

"I was all mixed up about him," Bonnie said. "I thought at first he was a white boy with a lot of sun tan. Then he looked like a colored boy till I got this close. All that was before I could tell he was an Indian boy. He could almost pass for white. I bet he'll try to do that sometime—he could get away with it right now after sundown."

Bonnie came even closer after that and the water was still not much above her waist. By that time she knew we were not standing up straight even though the river water was not clear enough for her to see that we were down on our knees.

"Uh-huh! I know now," Bonnie said, laughing at us. "You thought you had me fooled, didn't you? But I caught on. You're bashful. Both of you. You're not standing in a deep hole. You stripped off your clothes and came swimming naked. That's why you're hiding under water. You're trying to keep me from seeing you with nothing on. That's not a nice way to treat me. You don't want me to think you don't like me, do you, Steve?"

Duke was splashing in the water behind me. When I turned and glanced at him, he was crawling farther out into the river.

I felt the tight grip of Bonnie's hand on my shoulder

and an instant later she had pulled me around until I was facing her. After that she leaned over me and I could feel her hand moving down my chest and over my stomach. Then with a tight grip on me, she pulled me to my feet and spread her legs around my hips and locked her arms around my neck. I put my arms around her and hugged her tightly and wanted to hold her close to me as long as I could after that. Her underclothes had been unfastened and I had seen them floating around us before she pressed her bare breasts tightly against my face. After that I could not see anything for a long time while her body was trembling and shaking and jerking up and down on me. It was not easy for me to get my breath, either, until the tension of her legs relaxed and her body became soft and motionless and felt as if she were floating in my arms.

2

I WAS STILL HOLDING Bonnie's warm soft body close to me when Duke began pulling me away. I wanted to tell him to leave me alone but, before I could say anything, he had pulled us apart.

"Steve—Steve! Let's hurry and get out of here!" he was saying fearfully. "Come on, Steve!"

He had gripped my arm with both hands and was pulling me toward the river bank.

"Hurry, Steve!" he urged me. "Those two men will be coming back here any second now—I just know they will—I've got that scared feeling about it—and they're mean-looking white men—I've seen their kind before. I don't want to be caught here naked—and the way that girl's doing—and you'd better watch out, too. I don't know what they'd do to you—they'd murder me! They know I'm no Indian boy and they don't want to see a naked colored boy where there's a naked white girl— that's something I was born knowing! Let's get our clothes on before something bad happens! Please listen to me, Steve!"

"You don't have to run away," Bonnie called to us. "Stay here and let's have a good time."

"Don't listen to her, Steve," Duke whispered.

Bonnie was beckoning with urging motions of her hands for us to come back.

"You don't have to be scared of Bubba and Billy Roy. It's all right. I'll tell them to leave you alone. Come on back where I am."

"Maybe you'd tell them that, but maybe they won't hear you," Duke said to her hurriedly. He was looking to see if the two men were on their way back from the lower end of the island where they had gone to talk to Guthry. "And I'm in a big hurry not to wait to find out, either."

"Don't worry about them. They get all the dates they want with me. They get one anytime they want it. They're not hurting. I'm telling the truth. I can have dates with anybody else I want to the rest of the time. Don't go away."

"Please, Steve! Don't listen to her!" Duke whispered, pulling my arm harder. "I know trouble when I hear it.

And it's double-trouble when I can see it, too. I don't want this to be my last day in this world. Please, Steve! Do what I say! Come on!"

I wanted to stay there with Bonnie, but I was afraid of the two men, too, and I was shaking just as much as Duke was. We kept on wading toward the river bank where we had left our clothes and were almost there when Bonnie called to us again. Looking back, I saw her standing knee-deep in the shallow part of the river and wringing the water out of her underclothes. With her long dark-brown hair and large rising breasts, she looked exactly like the picture of a naked girl on a calendar I had seen in a barbershop in Memphis only the week before.

"Wait a minute—Steve and Duke—both of you," she was saying. She began moving her hand over one of her breasts and looked at us with an appealing smile. "Don't go away now. Don't you like me? If you'll come back, I'll tell you something."

Duke began backing away.

"Don't you want to know what I want to tell you?"

I could hear Duke begging me not to listen to her.

Bonnie's dark-brown hair was still dry and she tossed it away from her face with a motion that did not stop until it had shaken her breasts and then her hips. It was as if the girl on the barbershop calendar had come to life.

"I could have a date tonight—if somebody wanted to. You won't have to be scared then. I could have two dates tonight. I know how to take care of everything. Let's have a good time tonight."

She tossed her hair back from her face again.

"Don't forget what I said about tonight," she told us. "I didn't know there'd be anybody else down here on the island. I thought it'd be just Bubba and Billy Roy and me. I'm glad I came now."

We heard somebody talking on the island not far away and Duke, leaping in long strides, was the first one out of the water. As soon as we could get our pants and shoes on, and putting on our shirts as we went, we started walking toward our camp in the clearing.

When we looked back the last time, we saw Bonnie raise both hands high over her head and wave to us.

"This's a dangerous way for a colored boy to live," Duke said as we went into the bushes and out of sight of Bonnie. After we had gone a few yards, Duke stopped and leaned against a tree as if he were exhausted from a long walk. "I know it's a dangerous way to live because sometimes I wake up in the middle of the night and worry about what would happen to me if some white men caught me being around a white girl when she was naked like Bonnie."

As though he were still exhausted, Duke sat down on the ground, then I sat down and leaned back against a tree.

"Maybe it's the truth that girl's a waitress in that cafe in Paxton the way she claims to be," he said presently, "but she sure acts like something else down here. I don't know exactly like what, though—she didn't say she wanted money or anything like that. But I know one thing, because I've had it happen. When colored girls take off all their clothes, you can't always be sure what they've got in mind. They can fool you about that. They're not always out for some money or a pretty present. Some of them will do it only because they want to show off naked and be told how good-looking they are—and will bat you down if you try to get to them for anything else. Some others do it to start a good time going—and give you hell if you don't do what they want. That's why it's not always easy to figure out what they've got in mind.

"Anyway, whatever that Bonnie is, she ought to know better than talk to a colored boy the way she did— and show herself to me like that, too. She knows I'm no Indian boy—she knows I'm colored—and that kind of going-on could be the end of me if those two mean-looking white men hear about it. That's the first time in my life I ever saw a white girl naked. And I don't expect to again, either—and live to tell about it. I won't say I've never seen plenty of colored girls like that—and I'm not planning to stop. But white girls are for you, Steve. Not me. I never want to get in the bad trouble I'd be in if I got caught only just looking. And if more than only looking—"

He stopped and listened for several moments. We could not hear the sound of anybody walking through the bushes or talking nearby.

"If I got caught by those two whites—like the way she climbed on you and did that—they wouldn't even wait till sundown to string me up on a rope or shoot daylight holes through me. It gets me worried now just to think about it. You go on back there if you want to, Steve. I'm going to use all the sense I've got in my head and stay right at the camp the rest of the time down here so I won't run into trouble. Why don't you go back there where she is, Steve, if you want to? I won't tell anybody where you went. If you never saw a girl naked all over before, now's your chance to go back and look some more."

I told Duke that Bonnie was not the first girl I had seen when she was not wearing any clothes.

This was a girl about my own age who lived on the same block where I lived in Memphis. She came out on the back porch of her house one day while I was walking through the alley on my way home from school—it was a warm Friday afternoon in April—and she was completely naked. I had seen her at school almost everyday, and on the street many times, too, and I knew her name was Margie, but I had never talked to her before that afternoon when she asked me where I was going. I was so surprised to see a girl who had no clothes on—and it was bright daylight too—that I stood there staring at her for such a long time that she came to the edge of the porch and asked me the same thing again.

When I told Margie that I was going home, she asked me why I had to be in such a big hurry. I opened the alley gate and went as far as the porch steps. Margie said her parents and two brothers had gone downtown to buy shoes and that she was all alone in the house and that I could come inside if I wanted to. I asked her what would happen if I went inside the house and she said I would have to go inside to find out. She moved backward into the hall while I was crossing the porch and then she went into the kitchen.

After I got to the kitchen, Margie locked the door and sat down on the kitchen table. She had long reddish hair that had been pinned on top of her head and that made her look much older than she was. Her small breasts had been powdered a gleaming white and she had smeared both nipples with a brownish coloring that looked like chocolate and the cleft between her legs had been colored a rosy red with something that looked like ordinary catchup.

Besides looking so grown-up, she was not at all bashful about my seeing her as she was. First, swinging her legs back and forth, she asked me if I thought she was pretty and attractive, and I said she was beautiful. Next, she asked me if I thought she was the prettiest girl in school, and I told her that she was the prettiest girl I had ever seen anywhere. She looked pleased when I told her that, and she said I could come closer and touch her anywhere I wanted to and kiss her all the way up and down.

I put my hands between her legs and then was soon feeling her breasts all over. Most of the white powder came off and my hands were sticky with chocolate and catchup and she giggled and squirmed and I was going to start kissing her when suddenly there was a noise on the front porch. Margie jumped off the table and unlocked the kitchen door and ran to her room as fast as she could, and it did not take me long to jump off the back porch and leap over the fence to get to the alley.

I saw Margie at school many times after that, and sometimes on the street, but she always pretended not to know me and was never on the back porch again when I went through the alley on my way home. Her family moved away at the end of that summer and I never saw her again.

3

"WELL, STEVE, ALL I can say is that you were mighty lucky to get away before they caught you," Duke said when I had finished telling him about Margie in Memphis. "That was as lucky as I was a while ago getting away from Bonnie before those two whites saw me. But I still feel shaky about it."

We got up and started walking toward our camp.

"I don't know why they do that—colored girls will too," Duke said. "They must be all the same. Maybe it's because all of them—white and colored—want somebody to admire them and say they look pretty in a natural state. And that's nothing to lie about—unless they're too skinny or fat. However, there's one big drawback to it. I've heard of people being beat up and even shot when they've been caught with a girl like that when she was showing off herself. And it'd been even worse for me if those two white men had seen me with Bonnie back there when she had no more clothes on than I did. I'm going to have bad dreams about that for I don't know how long. And I'd bet a dime I'll have the first bad dream about it starting tonight."

When Duke and I got back to the clearing, the two men from Paxton—Bubba Youngblood and Billy Roy Smith—were raising and staking a canvas lean-to not far from our sleeping tent. Evidently they had rented a skiff from Clyde Owens to bring their camping equipment to the island, because they had a pile of quilts and cooking pans and other supplies at the end of the clearing. Troy Pickett had got up from his nap and he was watching them put up their lean-to.

It was late in the afternoon then and the sun was going down over the river in a fiery-red glow. A mild breeze was coming up the river and the heat of the day lingered in a comfortable warmth. The chirping birds were already coming back to the island and fluttering at their roosting perches for the night. It was time for the mosquitoes to come out and Duke threw some more driftwood on the smudge so the smoke would keep them away from us.

We had been expecting Guthry to stop fishing and come back to the camp any minute, but it was long after sunset before he got there. As he was walking toward us, we saw that he had not caught a single fish all afternoon and had even thrown away his fishing pole and bait can. However, he was smiling and puffing on his cigar as though contented and pleased about something.

"How was the swimming this afternoon, Duke?" he asked casually. "I heard a lot of splashing up there off and on so it must've been good for cooling off, anyway."

Duke nodded several times but said nothing.

"Well, Steve," Guthry said then, throwing a stick of wood on the smudge and sitting down with us in front of the tent, "this's been a real fine camp-out and I'm proud of myself for bringing you down here. It's been a man's kind of life and you won't forget it soon back in Memphis or anywhere else. Maybe you'll always remember how fried river catfish and red whiskey and a smoky campfire all go together so good. It's the finest combination I know of. But if you ever find a better combination be sure to let me know. In the meantime, though, since I'm proud of myself about it, I don't mind bragging a little. If you didn't have an uncle like me, I don't know how else you'd ever learn about living like a man in this world. What do you think, Steve?"

I told him that I had never known that a place like Summertime Island existed anywhere in the world and that I wished I could stay there until I had to go back to school at the end of summer.

Guthry got up and tossed several more pieces of driftwood on the smudge.

"I know how you feel, Steve," he said. "I feel the same way. And the trouble is that it's bound to come to an end like all good things have a way of doing too soon. We can't even stay one more day. Other people have moved in now and that makes it too crowded for comfort on this tiny little island—it wasn't made for more than three or four people at a time. We can't put up a fence between us and those others and somebody would be stepping on somebody else's toes in no time at all. I wish we could've stayed here one more day as we planned from the start.

"But that won't do now. I wouldn't want to stay here after tonight and risk having disagreements with those other people—that'd spoil the whole trip for us. We'll go out there to the narrows before it gets too dark and take down our trotline and have a last good catfish supper with the big catch we ought to have on it now—if somebody doesn't go out there and poach on our trotline before we get there. Then in the morning we'll get up at dawn and take our things across the backwater to the boat landing so we can make an early start. Even then it might take us all day to get back home. There's been more rain since we came down here and those mud holes can be just as miry as ever."

Guthry puffed thoughtfully on his cigar before saying anything more. Then with a quick glance, he looked at the two men in front of their lean-to. They had started a smudge and were tossing driftwood on it.

"By the way, Steve," Guthry said in a casual manner after several moments, "maybe you and Duke don't know about it, but I took a walk up the river bank a while ago to the upper end of the island. I wasn't catching any fish and so just before sundown I threw my pole into the river and went up where I thought you might still be swimming. And when I got there, it was a big surprise to see a girl come wading out of the water. She said she came down here with those two men from Paxton—they'd told me earlier that their names are Bubba Youngblood and Billy Roy Smith. I'd heard of them before—they've got a reputation all the way from

Paxton to Unionville for not being easy to get along with. Well, I thought I'd better tell you this.

"Anyway, it was a big surprise to see this girl up there because I never expected to see a woman on the island—not many of them want to come down here and put up with this kind of rough living. And I don't suppose she expected to see me, either. Well, because she wasn't wearing as much as a bathing suit of any kind. And as I said, she'd been wading in shallow water and was just coming out when I got there. I started to leave right away, because I thought she'd be embarrassed—you know, being naked like that—but she called me back and said she wanted to tell me something. I suppose I was the one who was embarrassed in the beginning, because she came on out of the water and was very friendly from then on. That's about all there is to say about it, I guess."

Duke had been glancing at me during all the time while Guthry was talking about Bonnie as if wondering if we should say anything ourselves about her. I shook my head everytime he looked at me.

"Well, now, on my way back down here," Guthry began talking briskly, "I decided we'd better pack up and leave the first thing in the morning. That's the sensible thing to do. Bubba Youngblood and Billy Roy Smith brought that girl down here with them—and with the four of us—well, that'd be six men and one girl like her on this tiny little island, and that kind of situation—"

He looked across the clearing at the two men in front of the lean-to.

"Well, there could be trouble in a case like that. Bad

trouble, too. When there's one woman as young and pretty as she is—and too many men around—that's how trouble will start. Those two men over there are rough and tough—they'd have to be to run a big sawmill and boss a cross-tie plant for the railroad. They're the kind who're not easy to get along with even when they're not mad about something. I found that out when they came down to where I was fishing and said they wanted to know how soon we'd be leaving and getting out of their way so they'd have the whole island to themselves. That's the way they talk. And if we stayed here and they caught one of us being too friendly with Bonnie—that's the girl's name, by the way. I forgot to tell you that a while ago and I—"

Guthry stopped abruptly and puffed nervously on his dead cigar several times while looking at the canvas lean-to. He had to strike a match and light the cigar again.

The two men had gone out of sight, but Troy Pickett, who had been talking to them, was walking toward us.

"To tell the truth," Guthry said quickly, "I'm already worried. That girl might tell them something—that I was up there where she was—she might tell them before we can get away from here."

Troy came over to our smoldering fire and leaned over to spit on it several times.

"Howdy, Troy," Duke said to him. "It's real friendly not to have to call you Mister Troy anymore."

Troy pretended not to have heard him.

"Troy!" Duke said then, speaking louder. "Don't spit out our smudge and let the mosquitoes in!"

Turning and glaring at Duke, and mumbling to himself, Troy then walked away.

"Come on, Duke," Guthry said, getting to his feet. "Let's go out to the trotline and bring in our catch before it gets too dark—or before some other people beat us to it. I know it's time for a good big drink of whiskey but we'd better go get our fish first. I've heard of people doing it the other way around—and getting so drunk they throw the fish away and swallow the hook themselves."

EIGHT

1

IT WAS LATE IN THE EVENING when we had finished
eating supper around the campfire and the moon came
up about the same time. It was a half moon with a
faint haze around it and there were scattered puffywhite
clouds drifting over the eastern horizon.

However, even then there was enough moonlight for
us to see the three people from Paxton moving around
their lean-to at the other end of the clearing. There
was loud talking and swearing and laughing and bang-
ing on pans while they cooked something to eat. We
had not seen the two men do any fishing that afternoon,
or had they taken any fish from our trotline, and evidently they were content to open cans of beef stew and
baked beans and drink whiskey for their supper.

After the heat of the day, it was comfortably warm
and balmy on the island. An upriver breeze kept the
smell of the backwater slough away from us—which

Duke called an unholy stink—and occasionally the wind was forceful enough to rustle the dark-green leaves of the willows. The croaking frogs had quieted down to a soft murmur and even the sound of water lapping on the riverbank was faint and gentle. Whiffs of woodsmoke from the smudges and campfires hovered around us as though trying to warn us that we were going to be sorry if we left Summertime Island and went home the next day.

Probably because it was our last night on the island, and not wanting to leave the next morning, nobody was sleepy or felt like going to bed. We sat around our campfire and listened to Guthry tell about some of his experiences as a traveling salesman before he married Aunt Rosemary and settled down and opened his hardware store in Unionville. It was the first time I had ever heard him talk about his life as a traveling salesman.

After one bottle of bourbon had been passed around and then thrown away empty, Duke got another one from the croker sack. Everybody had a tin cup and could help himself when the bottle was handed to him.

Guthry for many years had been a traveling salesman with a territory covering all of West Tennessee and part of Middle Tennessee as far as Nashville and called on retail dealers with a line of hard goods and farm supplies. Most of the stores were in small towns surrounded by farming communities and he traveled on trains and slept in drummer hotels and lived out of a suitcase and went back to the home office in Memphis for only one day every two weeks. In those days, Guthry said, the best demand was for one-horse plows, crosscut saws, and wash tubs, and long before farmers began buying tractors and power tools and refrigerators—and washing machines for their wives.

"And I'll tell you," Guthry said, "after a few years on the road you got the feeling that life wasn't anything but a constant string of gloomy Sundays in a drummer hotel with nothing to do except maybe play solitaire or swap tales with other sad-faced salesmen from Saturday afternoon to Monday morning."

As Guthry explained it, the reason he left the road and opened his own hardware store with the money he had saved was because Aunt Rosemary said she was too young and eager for company to marry a traveling salesman and then sit at home alone at night and be miserable for two weeks at a time while he was going around the country consorting with other women in hotels and whorehouses and such places whenever he felt like it. Aunt Rosemary's father owned a hardware and farm supply store in a small town in Middle Tennessee, which was where Guthry met her, and when he asked her to marry him, she told him that she had learned too much listening to traveling salesmen while clerking in her father's store and was too wise to marry him unless he promised to leave the road and stay at home with her.

Guthry poured another drink of bourbon into his tin cup and lighted a fresh cigar. The mosquitoes had come close again and Duke threw some more driftwood on the smudge to smoke them away. Troy, sitting nearby, was leaning back against a tree where he could watch Bonnie whenever she came into sight at the other camp. Instead of her pink dress, Bonnie was wearing what looked like either a skimpy two-piece bathing suit or her underwear. Whatever it was, it was constantly slipping farther and farther downward from her breasts and hips and she did not bother to keep herself completely covered.

"A lot of people thought traveling salesmen were walking devils who spent half their time swapping tales—when they weren't in a whorehouse," Guthry said. "And that wasn't far from the truth, either, when I was on the road. Besides that, most of the tales were about salesmen and women—and it was as much their stock-in-trade as notions and shoes and hardware or whatever goods they were peddling. Many salesmen specialized in certain kinds of tales and storekeepers got so they expected one of those salesmen to have a new story or joke every time before trying to write up orders.

"There've been hundreds and hundreds of stories and jokes about a traveling salesmen and the farmer's daughter, or any small-town girl—and they were usually as funny—and as dirty—as you can get. There were unending variations of the story about the blind girl who was too bashful to undress in front of a man until the lights were turned off, the one about the fat man who stopped a skinny girl on the street and asked her if she could change a five-dollar bill, and about the preacher's daughter who married a traveling salesman and forgot to take a nightgown on her honeymoon, and on and on by the dozens. Some of them took five or ten minutes to tell with all the extra details and others were ten-second snappies. I must have heard them all when I was on the road—and told them to storekeepers myself when I wanted to soften them up and get them in a good mood so I could write up some big orders.

"That is, I thought I knew all the stories till one I'd never heard before was acted out right in front of me. What was different about this one was that it wasn't either funny or dirty—it was sad. Tragic and sad. I often wish I could've done something about it instead of just standing there and watching it take place. But that's always the trouble when you regret something. If you don't act fast in a case like that, afterward it's forever too late. And after all this time I still can't keep it out of my mind."

Guthry was silent for several moments as he stared at the smoky smudge.

"This was at a little town down in the cotton-and-corn farming and dairy country near Jackson," he said, nodding slowly to himself as he began, telling about the incident in a subdued voice. "I'd finished my business for the day and had written up some pretty good orders —shovels and hoes and assorted wrenches and usual items like that. I was waiting in the railroad station to take the train to the next town on my regular route.

"I was feeling fine and calculating how much commission I'd made that day and speculating about how much my expense account would carry me when I got to where I was going that night so I could have a couple of drinks and spend a few dollars otherwise. It was after dark—around seven o'clock at night—and it was wintertime with frost on the waiting-room windows and a feel of snow in the air. There were five or six other passengers waiting for the same train—all of us were commercial travelers, as we liked to call ourselves—and every once in a while some of us would go to the big-bellied coal stove in the middle of the waiting room and warm our backsides. If you got ten feet away from the stove, you'd start shivering and shaking in no time—that's how cold it was. And as everybody knows, when it gets cold and frosty in Tennessee, you might as well be in Alaska.

"At the end of the business day like that, nobody was interested in telling jokes or listening to them, or had much to say about anything, while waiting for the train. Like I said, that's when salesmen were thinking about commissions and expense accounts and what they were going to do when they got to the next town for the night.

"It was still about twenty minutes before the train was due to arrive when a frightened-looking girl who was probably eighteen years old came into the depot waiting room. She was alone and she just stood there for a while, holding a small satchel, as if she had never been in a railroad depot before and did not know what to do. Finally, she saw the station agent's window and she went up to it and bought a ticket to go somewhere. Clutching the ticket in her hand then, she went to a bench in the farthest corner of the waiting room and sat there trembling and shaking in a thin, frayed, gray jacket with her arms locked tightly around her waist. If she had been shivering with cold, she could have gone to the stove and warmed herself like the rest of us were doing, but she appeared to be too frightened and timid to leave the corner where she was and go near anybody.

"This was a real good-looking girl with bright blue eyes and abundant blond hair and a girlishly slender body, but the frightened expression on her face made her appear to be a lot older than she could have been. Judging by the plainness of her clothes and shoes and her shyness, she looked like a farm girl who was going somewhere alone on a train for the first time in her life. Knowing the breed of traveling salesmen as I did, I was wondering which one of them would be the first to walk over to the corner and ask her if she were going to the same town he was—and maybe to the same hotel, of course. And so there were half a dozen traveling salesmen and one farmer's daughter—that's what I thought she was while I was watching her—and there was no limit to what you could imagine might happen after that. However, the way it turned out, she was a farmer's wife—not a farmer's daughter—and a runaway farmer's wife besides.

"Well, what happened was that a little while after this girl bought a train ticket and sat down in the far corner of the waiting room—and before any of the salesmen tried to talk to her—a man about forty years old, who was wearing farmer's dirt-stained overalls and heavy plow shoes, came into the depot waiting room and went straight to the girl. She began trembling violently and tried to shield herself with the small satchel.

"Without saying a word to her, the man knocked the satchel away and hit her on the side of her head with his open hand. The blow knocked her down on the bench, her ticket falling on the floor, and then he grabbed her arm and jerked her to her feet. She cried out, begging him not to hit her again, but that did not stop him from hitting her with his open hand once more.

"The first two salesmen who tried to help the girl were shoved away, and then the man took a pistol from his pocket and threatened to shoot anybody who came close to him after that.

"When you think about it afterward, six or seven men should've been able to handle one man even if he did have a gun. But when a strange man is in a rage and points a pistol at you, you're not likely to risk being shot and killed. However, while he was jerking the girl's arm and pulling her across the waiting room to the door, somebody did ask him why he was treating her the way he was doing. All he'd say was that anybody would do the same thing if his wife was trying to run away and leave him and go home to her parents. One of the salesmen went back to the bench to get the girl's ticket and small satchel for her. Everything in the satchel had spilled on the floor—a nightgown and a hairbrush and a box of talcum powder, and that was all.

"We followed them outside and watched the girl, clutching her satchel in one hand and the train ticket in the other, until she was taken out of sight in the night. She was still crying and begging not to be hurt anymore when the train whistle began blowing around the curve with such a piercing blast that no other sound could be heard."

"What happened then?" Duke asked.

"All of us went back for our sample cases and satchels and got on the train. And there weren't any jokes told in the smoker as usual, either, while we were riding to the next town. And ever since then when I hear stories about traveling salesmen and farmers' daughters—or farmers' wives—I always think of one that's not dirty and certainly not funny."

2

TROY STOOD UP, stretching himself and yawning.

"I'm a sonofabitch," he said after spitting at the campfire. "The next time if you want to tell a story that's my kind, Guthry Henderson, let me know and I might want to listen to it. I don't want to waste my time sitting around listening to no more like that one you took all that time to tell just now. Hell, when I go to church on Sunday, I have to sit there and hear the preacher tell that kind. But this ain't Sunday and the rest of the time I want to hear something rough and dirty."

"Troy—I know a funny story to tell you," Duke spoke up.

"Shut up, boy! Don't you talk to me!" He leaned forward to spit on the fire. "I don't want to hear nothing from you till you say my name right."

Troy had walked away and disappeared in the bushes when Bubba Youngblood came into the clearing from the lean-to and stopped halfway between the two campfires.

"Hey!" Bubba called out in a rasping loud voice. "Have you people seen Bonnie? Is she over there?"

Guthry told him that we had not seen her.

"Don't lie to me," he warned Guthry. "She went off somewhere a while ago. I went to sleep to take a little nap and I woke up just now and she's gone. She'd better not be hiding out over there. Billy Roy and me brought her down here for us and I don't want nobody else sooking around with her. You hear? I mean it. I ain't joking one minute. I don't care who it is. I'll beat hell out of him. You'd better hear!"

"I heard you," Guthry told him.

Bubba came several steps closer to our campfire.

"Where's that other fellow? I only see two of you and the nigger. Where'd that other one go to?"

"Troy Pickett's around here somewhere. He was right here a few minutes ago."

"I don't give a goddam what his name is, but he'd better watch himself and stay away from her. Billy Roy and me didn't bring her down here for him or nobody else to sook around with—you bring your own women down here for that. If I caught her at it—I'd beat all hell out of her, too."

Guthry said nothing more and Bubba went back to the lean-to. We could see him walking up and down in the flickering light of the campfire.

"Bonnie! Bonnie!" he began shouting in an angry voice that could have been heard anywhere on the island. "Bonnie! Goddam you! Come back here! You'd better not sook around out there! If you don't do what I tell you, you'll wish you had when I get hold of you!"

He stood still for a while, listening for her to answer, before calling her again.

"Bonnie! Goddam you, Bonnie! I know you can hear me! You'd better come back here before I get mad at you! You know what I'll do to you when I'm mad! I'll slap your tits so hard they'll stay hindside-to the rest of your life!"

Bubba went out of sight then, tramping noisily through the bushes, and only a few moments later Bonnie came out of the darkness and went into the lean-to where Billy Roy had been stretched out on a cot during all that time. Through the open end of the lean-to we could see them sitting on the cot and lighting cigarettes.

It was long after midnight then and Troy still had not come back. The moon was almost overhead then and the drifting clouds had finally disappeared and there was a shiny brightness on the green leaves of the willows like the first light of dawn. Guthry said that the sun rose so early at that time of year it would be only a couple of hours before it was time to get up to pack and leave and that we ought to lie down and get some sleep while we could. In addition to taking down the sleeping tent and rolling it up, the cots and quilts had to be folded and the cooking pans put into boxes and then everything carried to the two skiffs.

Guthry, yawning sleepily and throwing his cigar stub on the smudge, was the first to go into the tent.

Bubba came back to the lean-to after a while and found Bonnie there and all was quiet after that. When it was evident that Bonnie was not being beaten as

Bubba had threatened to do, Duke and I decided to go inside the tent and lie down to get as much rest as we could.

It was about three o'clock in the morning then.

However, I could not go to sleep right away. My cot was near the open flap of the tent and I could look out and see a few dim stars but it was still too early for the first glow of daybreak.

I lay there for a while wide awake listening to Guthry snoring on the other side of the tent. And then Duke, whose cot was next to mine, began talking excitedly in his sleep. I had been thinking about Bonnie and being with her in the river that afternoon and I wondered if the reason Duke was talking in his sleep was because he was dreaming about her. I tried to hear everything Duke was saying, but he was mumbling so excitedly that I could understand only a few words now and then.

"They won't have mercy . . . let me go . . . I'm no Indian boy . . . I was born colored . . . I've got to run . . . run, nigger, run . . . one-two-three . . . white girl . . . all naked . . . bare naked . . . pretty white girl bare naked . . . so pretty . . . so naked . . . those mean whites . . . they'll kill me right here . . . I don't want to die . . . please, white girl . . . let me go . . ."

After a while I became accustomed to Guthry's snoring and Duke's talking in his sleep and I was beginning to feel drowsy. I had closed my eyes and was dozing off to sleep at last when somebody sat down on the cot beside me. The cot squeaked, sagging and tilting, and I was wide awake at once. Duke was still talking in his sleep but his mumbling had become indistinct and I could not understand anything he was saying.

At first I thought Troy had come back and had been stumbling around trying to find his own cot in the dark. Then that was when Bonnie leaned over me.

I could see Bonnie's face so plainly that I knew at once who she was. Instead of wondering why she was there, however, I recalled in a flash hearing all the threats that Bubba Youngblood had made when he was calling her earlier that evening. Above the sound of Guthry's snoring and Duke's talking, I was sure I could hear Bubba and Billy Roy running from their lean-to to our tent.

I had held my breath as long as I could when Bonnie moved closer and put her hands on my face and told me in a whisper not to say anything aloud.

3

INSTEAD OF HAVING on her dress or a bathing suit, or even underwear, Bonnie had a quilt over her shoulders and it had fallen open until she looked just as she was when I saw her the last time that afternoon at the riverbank. She leaned further over me, her long dark-brown hair falling on my face, and she was so close to me that I could feel her breath on my cheek.

"Which one are you?" she asked, her voice barely audible. "What's your name?"

I told her in a whisper.

"You haven't forgotten me so soon, have you, Steve?" she said, pressing her cheek on my face. "I'm Bonnie. You know. This afternoon. In the river."

Before I could say anything, she moved even closer. Her breasts were soft and warm.

"Don't be scared, Steve," she said. "Don't worry. I've got Bubba and Billy Roy asleep now. They won't be out looking for me now. Everything's all right now. There's nothing to worry about now."

Sitting up then, she swept her hair away from her face with a quick motion of her hands.

"How much longer are you going to be down here on the island?" she asked.

I told her that we were going to get up at dawn to go back to Unionville.

"Do you really have to go back so soon? Can't you stay longer?"

When I said that my uncle had decided to leave a day early, she was silent for a moment. The sounds Guthry and Duke were making seemed to be louder than ever.

"Which cot is he on?" she asked then. "You know. Up there swimming with you today. The one who looks like an Indian—the Indian boy. He gave me such a good shivery feeling—I can still feel it."

I pointed to the cot next to mine.

"I want to tell you something, Steve," she whispered. "I had a good time with you out there in the river. Let's have some more like that. Come to Paxton to see me anytime you want to. The Crystal Palace. We'll have

142

more good times. Don't forget me. I'll be looking for you. You'll be glad you did."

Bonnie pressed her cheek against my face once more. Then, holding the quilt over her shoulders, she got up and went to Duke's cot. He was no longer talking in his sleep then and may already have been awake. Anyway, instead of saying something in surprise, he did not make a sound when she got on the cot with him and leaned over him. The quilt fell from her shoulders and in the dim light I could see her getting closer to him.

All I could see of Duke at first was his face and then soon after that I saw him put his arms around Bonnie. Seeing him like that, all I could think of was how worried he had been that afternoon and fearful of Bubba and Billy Roy seeing him with her while he was naked and she had taken off her underclothes.

That was when I began to worry more than ever and I was thinking of all the trouble that could happen. Guthry was still snoring, but I expected somebody— Troy Pickett or Bubba or Billy Roy—to come running into the tent at any moment and seeing Bonnie and Duke on the cot. I was not as worried about what might happen to Bonnie as I was about Duke—I thought she would be able to take care of herself somehow but I knew something terrible would happen to Duke. Bonnie might say he was an Indian but the others certainly would not.

While I lay there dreading to hear the sound of footsteps and wondering what I ought to do, Duke's cot, with a splintering of wood and ripping of canvas, collapsed and crashed to the ground. When I looked to see what had happened, it was as if Bonnie and Duke did not even know the cot had collapsed.

Guthry suddenly stopped snoring and I could see him rise up and look around as if wondering what had awakened him. A few moments later he was sitting on the side of his cot and looking directly at me. Since Bonnie and Duke were on the ground behind my cot, they were out of his sight.

"Steve," Guthry called in a drowsy voice.

I did not answer him, thinking he might go back to sleep. However, after he had sat there for a few moments, I could see him putting on his shoes.

"Are you awake, Steve?"

When I still did not answer him, he struck a match to light the lantern.

"Steve!" he called out loudly. "What made that noise just now? Did you hear it?"

I told him that I had heard something.

Just as Guthry turned up the lantern wick and the light flared brightly, Bonnie got up, wrapping the quilt around her, and ran from the tent.

"Good God!" Guthry said. He was wide awake then. "That girl—she's the same girl—Bonnie—"

He came to the middle of the tent with the lantern.

"It was her—she's the only woman on the island— What was she doing here? Did you know about it? Those men from Paxton—Bubba and Billy Roy—"

Coming closer with the lantern then, he saw Duke on the broken cot behind me. Duke had wrapped his quilt around him but he was shaking and trembling as if it had been a cold night in midwinter.

"God Almighty—that's where she was! Duke! What in the world!"

Duke sat up and reached for his shoes.

"You know I couldn't help you if you got caught like that!" Guthry told him excitedly. "You know that, Duke! You—and a white girl!"

Duke was fumbling with his shoelaces. His hands were shaking so much that he could not even tie hard knots in them.

"I came here and went to sleep," Duke managed to say. "That's the truth—that's all I know—"

He was too frightened to say anything more.

"We've got to hurry and get off this island," Guthry told us, still looking at the broken cot. "We can't stay here a minute longer than we have to—it's too danger-ous. Let's hurry up and get this tent taken down and load up everything in the skiffs and get away from here as fast as we can. And I mean fast! Those two men—if they found out about it—that white girl and Duke—and if Troy Pickett—"

He turned and looked at Troy's cot.

"Where is he—where's Troy?"

I told him that Troy was still somewhere outside.

"That's good," Guthry said, relieved. "I'm glad to hear that. But don't say a word about this to Troy. Not a single word. Keep it from him. I know what he'd try to do if he found out about it."

We had folded three of the cots and rolled up all the quilts and were taking down the tent when Troy got there. Guthry had already thrown the broken cot on the campfire and it was beginning to blaze.

"I'm a sonofabitch," Troy said. "What the hell you all doing? I ain't been here to sleep yet tonight."

"And you won't—not here," Guthry told him. "We're packing up and leaving."

"What the hell for? It ain't even daybreak yet and I want my sleep."

"Everybody had a chance to sleep some tonight—you, too, Troy. Now it's time to pack up and go. It'll be daylight soon."

"What did you go and burn up that cot for?"

"It's too old and broken down to carry all the way back to Unionville."

"How come it got so old all of a sudden and went and broke down in the middle of the night?"

Troy looked at me, then at Guthry, and finally at Duke, but none of us answered him.

"There's something as funny as hell about this," he stated suspiciously. "I must've dozed off for a while when I was out there in the bushes on the watch for that girl and missed something that went on here. People don't burn up a cot in the middle of the night and leave this early for no good reason. Who was sleeping on that cot when it broke down?"

"Never mind about that now, Troy," Guthry told him shortly. "There's no time to talk. Pick up something to carry. We've got to hurry and load up the skiffs."

146

NINE

1

IT WAS A GRAY DAWN with thin streaks of motionless dark clouds above the southern horizon and the three people from Paxton, rolled up in quilts, were still asleep in the open-ended lean-to when we had carried everything to the skiffs and were ready to leave Summertime Island.

A fiery sun soon came up over the bluff behind Little Dipper Landing and then by the time we had rowed the loaded skiffs about halfway across the backwater the whole sky was being colored with a pale blue tint.

There was still a lingering coolness of night air and an early morning mist was slowly rising from the warm water and making little wisps of vapor looking like misshapen gray balloons that sparkled briefly in the sunlight just before suddenly vanishing as if they had never existed. In the calm air of early morning before the coming of daytime breezes, a long column of wood-smoke, looking as solid and motionless as a tall smokestack above a factory, went straight upward from the kitchen chimney of Clyde Owens' house.

There was nobody at the boat landing when we got there and began to unload the skiffs. In a little while, though, Clyde left his house and came down the grassy hummock to the mud flat. Guthry spoke to him right away, saying the day had started out being fine and sunny with no rain clouds in sight, but Clyde ignored Guthry and the rest of us and did not have a single word to say until he had carefully inspected his boats to see if we had damaged them. He knew the oar locks were loose and splintered when he rented the skiffs, but he made a big to-do of rattling them noisily anyway just as if we had broken them. He kicked at one of the skiffs with an angry fling of his foot.

"Looks to me like decent people would want to take better care of other folks' property when they're trusted with it," he said in a gruff fault-finding manner. "You didn't splinter no oars or lose none, and you didn't bust out no bottom boards, neither, but just look at all that mud you people tramped in those skiffs and didn't even bother to clean out.

"When I see people come down here to my boat landing and do something like that, what it makes me want to do is go to a man's house and track mud all over his floors and wipe my feet on his rugs. And if that wasn't enough, I'd wipe my shoes on his window curtains, too. It's too much bother to go to court and sue you this time, so I'll just remember your faces the next time you people come down here and want to rent from me. I won't forget what none of you look like and I'll either charge you double or won't rent at all. I ought've known by the looks of your faces when you got here this time to charge you double or not let you rent from me."

"I remember there was a lot of mud in those skiffs when we took them the other day, Clyde," Guthry told him. "They sure weren't spick-and-span."

"If that's your memory, then it ain't much if you can't even remember that you still owe me a dollar. Go ahead and remember that now."

"A dollar for what? I paid you the full rent you asked for at the start."

"A dollar to make me come down here to inspect before I could finish eating my breakfast. A man is entitled to sit in peace in his own house at breakfast time."

He took the dollar from Guthry and watched us until we had finished unloading the skiffs.

"Did you people take any of them catfish over there?" he asked after that in the same gruff manner. "Or didn't you never get your trotline up after all?"

Guthry told him that besides catching all we could eat, we had stopped baiting half of the trots because we were catching more catfish than we could use.

"Sounds to me like somebody stayed sober off and on then," Clyde said, looking at Troy. "I saw that big sack of whisky you took over there. I expected all four of you people to get drunk and fall in the river and never come up for air. That's the best thing that could happen to some people—it saves their wife going to all the trouble and expense of digging a grave and paying the undertaker. It looks to me like if a man wants to get stinking drunk he'd marry a woman who'd let him do it at home instead of her sending him down here on a fishing trip and giving my boat landing a bad reputation."

"You're a friendly sort of man, Clyde," Troy told him with a wide smile, walking up and slapping him on the shoulder. "I can tell that about you by the friendly way you talk so early in the morning. I sure do admire that. I'm a pretty good judge of people and you're the kind to make me feel mighty good about knowing you. You'd be the real neighborly kind to live next door to. I could live side-by-side with you all my life and never have a spat and falling out. That's something I can't say about nobody else I know. I'll be proud to know you all my life from now on."

"Well, I never was a real quarreling man," Clyde said. "Quarrelsomeness just ain't my nature."

"That's exactly how I had you figured out from the start," Troy told him.

Clyde, with a quick nod, began grinning good-naturedly for the first time.

"Well, there're some good people in this world—once you get to know them a little."

"I believe the same way, Clyde. That's what I always say. Now, if I could get a little drink of water, I'd sure appreciate it. I've been thirsty all morning. Reckon I could get a drink of water somewhere?"

"Sure," he said with no hesitation as if they had been lifelong friends. "You bet you can. You go up there on the back porch at my house and help yourself to all you want. That's where you'll find the water bucket. Right on the back porch."

Troy had left at once and was already at the hummock when Clyde suddenly turned and called to him in an anxious raising of voice.

"Now, help yourself all you want on the back porch," he told Troy. "But don't go on the inside of the house. You hear?"

Troy raised his arm and waved.

While we were carrying everything to the truck from the mud flat, Clyde had been busy pulling the two skiffs up the log skid. We were soon packed and ready to leave, but Troy had not come back.

As we waited, Clyde walked up to the truck. He had been there for only a few moments when he looked at us one after the other as if counting heads.

"Where's that other fellow?" he demanded. "Ain't he back yet from getting a drink of water?"

Without waiting for anyone to say something, he started running up the hummock to the house. When he got there, he went around the side of the house to the back porch. It was not long then until Troy, slamming the screen door behind him, came running from the front porch.

Clyde was right behind Troy but did not follow him all the way down the hummock. He stood up there shouting about something but, if he had been telling Betty to bring his pistol, she failed to do it.

"I'm a sonofabitch," Troy said, panting for breath, when he got to the truck. He was careful to watch Clyde on the hummock. "Did you see that? I was up there listening to her tell about how lonesome she gets down here where nobody's around much except her old man and she was getting willing for me just when her old man came busting in."

Clyde kept on shouting but Betty still had not come out of the house.

"Goddam it! I've been down here all this time for nothing," Troy was saying. "A goddam nothing. And last night on the island too—for nothing. That girl from Paxton was running all over the place and in and out of somewhere all night long but never nowhere where I could find her—like she didn't want to have nothing to do with me. I never could catch up with her last night. But somebody did, I'm goddam certain about that. And maybe everybody but me. That's what I'm thinking and it makes me suspicious as hell about what went on over there last night. I'll tell you one thing. If I knowed for sure—if I found out—if everybody else—"

He was glaring at Duke.

"What do you know about it—you nigger bastard!"

"Troy—" Duke began.

"Shut up! Shut your nigger mouth! Don't you never call me that no more. You ain't on that island now. If you want to say something to me—you call me Mister Troy. And I ain't forgetting all the times you didn't call me the way you ought to over there, neither. I'm going to pay you back good and plenty for every goddam time you done it and don't you forget it. You just wait a little while and see if I don't. I'll get you!"

"We want to be going, Troy," Guthry urged him, pushing Troy toward the driver's seat. "We don't want to stand here and waste time quarreling. It's getting late and it's a long way back to Unionville. Let's hurry and get started home."

"Goddam nigger bastard—that white girl—Bonnie—something went on there last night—if I'd caught—"

"And if you'd gone far enough to get that girl down up there in that house a while ago, and if Clyde Owens had caught you at it—"

"I ain't done yet. The day's not over. I'm not wasting all this time off on a fishing trip for nothing. Not me. I'd be ashamed to go back and show my face in Unionville if I done that."

2

DUKE AND I GOT INTO THE BACK of the truck and sat down on the pile of quilts. He was quiet as we sat there looking down the road behind us as the truck moved away from Little Dipper Landing and took us out of sight of Clyde Owens, leaving him standing in front of his house on the hummock.

I knew that Duke, just as I was, was thinking about the threats Troy had made and wondering what he might do. It was not likely that he would start another fist fight with Duke, and risk being forced to give up again, and he did not have a gun in the truck. However, Troy was the kind of person who, when he had built up a grudge, would generate intense anger and rage until he had an opportunity to retaliate with cruelty and violence. Both Duke and I knew that much about him after being in close company with him for only a few days.

We had left the bottomland and the tangled growth of trees, bushes, and trailing maypop vines and the truck was slowly grinding up the long winding grade to the top of the bluff. It was late in the morning already and, even if we did not get stuck in a mud hole, it would take most of the day for us to get to Unionville.

"The way Troy was talking back there at the boat landing—" Duke began saying and then quickly stopped to correct himself. "I mean Mister Troy. I've got to watch myself and get back in that habit. Mister Troy— Mister Troy. White man—Mister Troy. One—two— three—"

He gazed down the road behind us for a while.

"Well, the way he talked made me feel sorry we had to leave that island. It's like feeling homesick. I thought he and I would get along fine—after that tussle we had when I wrestled him down and he gave up. It was a real friendly feeling being there and talking to him and Guthry and you like I was just an ordinary person and no different than anybody else. It seemed so easy and natural to get along together that way. I didn't have to worry about being who I am and watching my talk to white people. Summertime Island. I'll never forget it—Summertime Island.

"I wish I could live all my life from now on at a place like that. Every time a white man jumps at me from now on about something, I'll have to do what he says and not talk back. Yes, sir. No, sir. Please, sir! But

I'll be thinking to myself how friendly it was down here and wishing I could come right straight back. It's a good thing I can think what I please even if I can't say it out loud. Summertime Island. That's the place for me."

He opened his tackle box and took out the geography textbook. Then he carefully turned the pages until he found the map he wanted to see.

"Steve, do you think there are other places anywhere else like that one?" he asked, holding his finger on the map where he thought Summertime Island would be if it had been large enough to be drawn on the map. "I mean, where it'd be friendly enough for colored people to live and not have to run scared all the time."

I told him that we would have to get a boat and go up and down the whole length of the Mississippi River to find out if there were other places on it like Summertime Island.

"I don't know if that would help any, though, even if we found some others like it," he said after thinking about it for a while. He shook his head slowly. "Every year when the spring floods came, they'd be under water and nobody could stay there. Maybe there is no place where the colored can go and live in a friendly way with white people all the time. Not right now that I know about. Most of the white people I know about don't want it that way. They want it like it is. But maybe someday. And I hope I can live that long for that great day to rise up with the sun."

Duke nudged me with his elbow.

"Steve, maybe you don't have anything against me

for being colored, but you can't know how it is for the colored without being colored yourself. You have to be born that way to know about it."

When we reached the top of the bluff, we saw the broad, winding, muddy Mississippi River for the last time. From that distance, Summertime Island looked so tiny that it was no more than a narrow sand bar with a scant covering of green willows and even the back-water slough appeared to be no larger than a pond in a cowpasture. Whatever it was that Duke was thinking about while he was looking down at the island, it brought tears to his eyes and he had to wipe them away with the back of his hand.

After that the dirt road was straight and flat and, since it had not rained during the night to make the road slick with mud, Troy began driving the truck as fast as it would go. We soon passed Hugh Huffman's store at the fork of the road without stopping to buy anything to eat and went about two miles farther to-ward Unionville before we had to slow down at a mud hole.

Troy was able to get the truck through the first mud hole, but a few minutes later it bogged down axle-deep in a larger one. Duke and I, as well as Guthry, got out and pushed until Troy was able to get the truck to the other side of it.

By then it was about the middle of the afternoon and the sun was hot and we were hungry. Guthry opened the last cans of baked beans and we sat on the side of the road in the shade of some oak trees and ate from the cans with our spoons. Troy grumbled because there was no more bourbon left and he said that the first thing he was going to do when he got to Unionville was to make up for it in a hurry.

While the rest of us were taking our time about eating, Troy hurriedly finished his can of beans. He tossed the empty can into the ditch and then got up and went into the sapling grove by the roadside. There was a large farm behind the grove where a work gang of ten or twelve Negro girls and older women were hoeing field rows and we had heard them talking and laughing ever since we had pushed the truck out of the mud hole and stopped to eat.

It was not long after Troy had gone into the grove when there was a sudden end to the sound of laughter in the field behind it. We could not see through the grove of saplings, but presently we heard one of the Negro women cautiously ask Troy why he was there.

We could not hear what Troy said but, whatever it was, it frightened the women because we could hear distinctly the excited voice of one of them.

"Go away from here, white man," she told him. "We don't want you bothering us. You leave us alone. Go on about your business somewhere else. We don't want nothing to do with you."

"You'd better watch how you talk to me," Troy said. "You don't know who I am."

"White man, get away from us," she told him angrily. "It makes no difference who you is. We don't work for you and don't have to listen to you. You go on away from here now."

"Shut up," Troy told her.

"If you want me to shut up, you quit bothering that girl like that. Turn her arm loose and leave her alone. You hear?"

In another moment several of the women were talking excitedly.

"You'd better quit that what you're doing, white man!" one of them said. "Leave her alone!"

"Nigger, if you hit me with that hoe, I swear to God I'll grab it and beat hell out of all of you with it. Now stand back out of my way."

"Please, white man, go on off and leave us alone."

"You mind your own business," he told her.

"I'm minding my own business—the colored folks' business. You go off somewhere after your own kind—leave our kind alone. We don't want nothing to do with you. Let go of that little girl."

"I'll knock hell out of you, nigger, if you don't shut your mouth and get out of my way. I ain't fooling about what I say."

"Please, sir, white man," one woman begged, sobbing loudly. "Don't do that. That's my little girl. She's too young and little. You can see how young and little she is. Lord have mercy!"

"White boss, please get somebody else—anybody else will do," another woman said pleadingly. "Leave that poor little girl alone. Don't take her off to those bushes. She's so young and little for you to do that. Please take somebody else off—if you've got to—anybody else—not her!"

"To hell with that," he said. "I know what I want."

"Let me go with you, please, white boss—I'll go—I'll

do anything you say—I promise you—please don't take
my little girl!"

3

THE WOMEN WERE WAILING in the field and closer to us
we could hear Troy tramping in the underbrush as he
came back into the sapling grove. Presently we heard
the shrill cry of a girl's voice.

Guthry stood up. "Troy! Troy Pickett!" he shouted.
"Come here! You hear me, Troy!"

After having called several times more, Guthry began
walking up and down beside the drain ditch. All three
of us had left the shade and were out in the sun with
the dripping sweat of the afternoon heat on our faces
and trickling under our shirts.

There was no end to the moaning and wailing of the
Negro women in the field. Some of them began chanting
a mournful song of grief.

"What can anybody do?" Guthry said presently, stopping and looking at Duke. "He's Troy Pickett. He won't
listen to me. And if I went in there now and tried to
stop him, he'd build up a grudge against me and never
get over it. He killed a man once for less than that."

With a helpless expression on his face, Duke was
slowly shaking his head.

"He's already got a whopping big grudge against me.
For that wrestling him to the ground till he had to give
up and then not calling him Mister Troy on the island.

And about what he thinks he knows about what happened last night in the tent. He'd kill me for sure if I went in that grove now and said the least little word to him about letting that little colored girl go."

Guthry leaned against the side of the truck and wiped the sweat from his face. We could hear one of the Negro women praying above the chanting and wailing.

"Steve," Guthry said after a while, speaking slowly and looking down the road toward the river and Summertime Island, "Steve, I didn't know there'd be things like this going on when we started out on this fishing trip. I made a big speech about how much good it'd do you at your age to get away from homefolks for a few days and learn about growing up with men. And I was boasting about what a great thing it was for you to have an uncle who'd take you on a camp-out down on the river. I won't take any of that back, and all I can say now is that it sure wasn't planned the way it's turned out.

"I'll be truthful about it, Steve. The way it started out was that I needed a good excuse to tell your Aunt Rosemary so I could get away and come down here myself. She knows men don't spend all their time fishing on a camp-out—there's bound to be some crap shooting or drinking or going after girls, and women don't like to stay at home and know damn well some or all of that is going on for four or five days at a time. Of course, I wanted you along. That was as much of it as anything else. I'm sure the only reason your Aunt Rosemary was so agreeable and willing to run the store for me and let us spend all this time away from home was because she thought I'd behave myself if you went along.

"Now, that's why if she asks you too many questions, the less you have to tell her the better it'll be. Just hesitate to say more than you have to and let me do most of the talking about it. If she asks you outright about certain things, you could say that I'd know more about it than you do. That's being truthful, because I always try to explain things to her so she'll understand better. It's not that I want to hide anything in particular from her—it's just that I'd want things explained the way I think they ought to be from my point of view.

"For instance, I didn't know that girl—Bonnie—would be on the island the same time we were—it was just like she'd dropped out of the blue sky. I never was more surprised in my life. And I never thought anything like this—about Troy Pickett now—would happen, either. It's easy for a woman like your Aunt Rosemary to misunderstand how unexpected things like that can happen and get real upset like women will do.

"Looking at it another way, though, it's been a good education for you to learn firsthand about people when you're at your age and not have to get rid of your ignorance when you're older. Or else wait too long and never get rid of it as it happens to some people—that's when prejudice sets in and gets a lifetime grip on you. Anyhow, you learned a lot about trotline fishing and a river camp-out and that's what we went down there for. I can be proud of that if nothing else. And maybe the way it turned out the best of all was making friends with

Duke Hopkins. You could never turn against Duke—or any fine colored fellow like him—after this."

We had been there long enough for the sun to begin going down behind the treetops when Troy Pickett came out of the grove. The mournful wailing and chanting of the Negro women gradually sounded farther and farther away and we could see them going slowly homeward across the field toward a row of darkly weathered log cabins about a quarter of a mile in the distance. The young girls ran ahead, leaving the older women to trudge wearily over the plowed ground.

"I'm a sonofabitch," Troy said with a pleased grin and talking in a boastful loud voice as he looked at Duke. "What'd I tell you, nigger? Remember what I said back at the boat landing when Clyde Owens chased me out of his house before I could drop my pants and shoot my pecker? Well, all I had to do was hold back my pecker and get to this place to drop them for a good-looking little high-yellow. And when I can have my pick, I'll pick one of them every time. I didn't spend all my time on this trip for nothing, did I, nigger? What do you think about that?"

Duke, taking a step backward and shaking his head slightly, said nothing.

"What makes you so shut-mouth about what I done? Because I went after one of your kind? Hell, how do you figure you got to be half white and half black yourself? You think God done it just for a special favor to you? Is that what makes you act so stuck-up?"

Duke still made no reply.

"Goddam, if that's what you think, you'd be blue-black and kinky-haired yourself right now instead of a half-and-half mulatto bastard or whatever kind of nigger bastard you think you are."

"Come on, Troy," Guthry urged him, trying to pull him to the truck. "Let's go home. There're more sink holes to get through between here and Unionville and the sun's going down fast. I don't want to have to get out and slop around in that mud after dark. We're wasting time here. Start the truck and let's get going."

Troy jerked his arm from Guthry's grip and went back to Duke.

"Why can't you say something when I talk to you? You ain't deaf and dumb."

"Yes, sir, Mister Troy."

"You didn't say it like that down on the island, though, did you, nigger?"

"No, sir, Mister Troy."

"You think you're better than me?"

"No, sir, Mister Troy."

"You want to know what I think of you?"

"Yes, sir, Mister Troy."

Troy drew back his fist and hit Duke as hard as he could on the face. Duke stumbled backward several steps but did not fall down. A slow trickle of blood began running down his chin from his lip.

"Now, start talking, nigger," Troy ordered. "And talk fast. And I don't want to hear no lies, neither. Go ahead. Say it. What do you know about that white girl down there last night?"

"Leave him alone, Troy," Guthry told him. "That's enough of it."

Getting a grip on Troy's arm with both hands, Guthry pulled him to the truck.

"You've already had one fight with Duke," Guthry said, "and there's no sense in starting another one no matter who wins it. I won't stand for it. And I mean it, too. Now, let's go home."

Troy jerked his arm free and climbed into the truck to start the engine.

"I ain't done with him yet!" we could hear him shout above the noise of the engine. "I'll get him! He'll find out!"

Duke and I ran and climbed into the back of the truck as it began moving up the road.

TEN

1

IT WAS IN THE MIDDLE OF THE MORNING, nine o'clock or later, and the sun was already shining through the open window with the bright daytime heat of June when I got out of bed to begin putting on my clothes. The evening before, I had gone to bed without nightclothes because it had been too hot to wear anything.

After sleeping on a narrow cot in the tent for nearly a week, and getting up at dawn or earlier every day, it felt strange to wake up in a soft wide bed between clean white sheets instead of being rolled up in a smelly damp quilt and to see pictures on the walls around me and to look up at a white ceiling instead of at mildewed gray canvas.

While getting dressed, I still felt drowsy and could have stayed in bed and gone back to sleep at once if the sun had not been shining full in my face. There were no sounds anywhere in the house and I wondered if Aunt Rosemary had gone down to the hardware store with Guthry. It was Saturday and he had said at supper the night before that he was going to open the store early in the morning and be ready for a good day's business.

I had been awake probably for two or three hours during the night, and I was sure that was the reason why I had overslept that morning. I had asked Guthry to wake me up early so I could go down to the store with him to unpack the freight shipments that Troy Pickett's brother had delivered while we were away, but evidently he thought I needed more sleep and did not want me to get up as early as he did.

Whether or not it was because I felt so drowsy, I was in no hurry to finish getting dressed and I sat on the side of the bed and thought about what had taken place during the night. At first I tried to think of it having been only a dream, but I could remember so clearly everything that had taken place that I knew it had to be real.

What had happened was that Aunt Rosemary came into my room in the middle of the night and sat down on the bed beside me. When she woke me up, she had her hand over my mouth and was leaning over me and whispering that she wanted me to be quiet and not talk loudly enough to wake up Guthry in the bedroom across the hall.

Suddenly waking up like that in the middle of the night, I had no idea why she was there. For the next several moments I stared at her wonderingly and waited for her to tell me why she had waked me up.

There was enough moonlight for me to see that she was not wearing either a dress or a bathrobe and that the deep opening of her nightgown was unfastened from her neck almost to her waist. Leaning closer and whispering with her hand still over my mouth, she said something about Bonnie.

The evening before while we were eating late supper—Guthry and I had got home about eight o'clock—Aunt Rosemary had managed to find out by constantly questioning Guthry that there had been a girl on Summertime Island the night before we left there. After finally saying that much, all Guthry would tell her then was that the girl's name was Bonnie and that she was a waitress and that she was camping there with two men from Paxton. Aunt Rosemary had been persistent and cajoling after that, and even sat on Guthry's lap and put her arms around his neck, but he kept on telling her there was nothing more he could say about it.

When she could not get him to say anything more, Aunt Rosemary had asked me what I knew about Bonnie while we were on the island. Just as Guthry had said he wanted me to do, I told her that he would know more about Bonnie than I did. My saying that made her more curious and suspicious than ever from that moment on and she stated that she was not going to be satisfied until she found out exactly what she wanted to know and would not stop at anything until she knew what had actually taken place on the island.

Aunt Rosemary was so upset and provoked with Guthry then that she said he must have had a very convenient loss of memory and imagined he was an unmarried traveling salesman again and could go around the country sleeping with this-that-and-the-other woman whenever he felt like it. When I went to bed as soon as I had finished eating supper, she and Guthry continued talking in loud voices in their room and I could still hear her asking questions when I was falling asleep.

I had been so startled when Aunt Rosemary woke me up in the middle of the night and began whispering to me that I did not realize how close she was to me until I felt the softness of her body through her thin nightgown and could see the whole fullness of her large round breasts in the dim light. I had a sudden stiffening of my body and felt a throbbing urge for her body and wished she had been Bonnie or some other girl I could hug in my arms.

"Steve, I want to know more about that girl on the island," she said in a whisper. Her voice was tense but there was a softness about it that I had never heard before. She put her hand on my cheeks and neck at first, and then her hand moved downward over my chest until she was gently stroking the whole throbbing stiffness of my body. It made no difference to me then that she was Aunt Rosemary—she could have been Bonnie or any other girl in the warm moonlight. "Tell me all about it, Steve. What did you do? Did you make love to her? Don't be afraid to tell me. It's all right. You can tell me. I want to know all about it. Was she pretty and attractive? How old was she?"

Since it had been such a hot night I had gone to bed without wearing nightclothes, but I did have a sheet over me. I was already so excited by the stroking of her hand that I would have told her anything she wanted to know about Bonnie, but, before I could say a word, she jerked the sheet away. I could see her looking at me and I could feel the faster stroking of her hand and I was glad I was naked and I wanted her to be naked too. That was when she moved over me and began squeezing and rubbing and kissing me as no girl had ever done to me before.

I could wait no longer. I jerked her nightgown over her head, ripping it as it went, and threw it away so I could kiss her breasts one after the other and time after time and then locked my arms around her so I could feel the throbbing sensation of the excited twisting and thrusting of her body on me. I did not know how long a time it had lasted, but I held her in my arms as long as I could after that until she drew away, trembling slightly as she breathed deeply, and lay close beside me on the bed.

She was quiet and still for a while until she began talking in a calm whisper.

"Steve, did Bonnie make love to you like that?" she asked, pressing her cheek against my face. "Or was it some other way? Tell me all about it, Steve. Was she good to you? There's nothing to be bashful about. It's all right. You can tell me."

I felt then as if I could talk to her just as if I were saying it to myself. I told her about Bonnie wading into the river while Duke and I were swimming and how she had taken off her underwear and put her arms and legs around me. Then I told her how Bonnie had said Duke looked like an Indian and not a colored boy and wanted him to stay in the water with her but that he was afraid of being seen by the two white men from Paxton.

"What about anybody else?" she asked quickly. "Who else did she make love to beside you? Was she after everybody else too?"

I knew that if I told her that Bonnie came into our tent while we were asleep and got on the cot with Duke that she would ask if Bonnie was also on Guthry's cot. Although I could tell her truthfully that I had not seen Bonnie with Guthry on his cot, I knew she was determined to keep on trying to find out if Guthry had been with Bonnie either in the tent or somewhere outside. While I waited and tried to think what to tell her, she pulled me closer and once more stroked me with the soft clinging pressure of her hand.

"You haven't told me everything I want to know, Steve," she whispered. "And you haven't made love to me, either. Don't you want to?"

She must have known that I wanted her just as much as ever, and when I hesitated, she whispered to me again and told me not to be afraid. And when I moved to her, she reached to me helpfully with both hands and said over and over it was what she wanted me to do and not to be afraid to do anything I wanted to do. I was clinging to her and had been gripping the warm softness of her body when suddenly she bit me so painfully that I had to hit her with a shove of my arm to make her stop before I had to yell with the pain of her bite.

2

AFTER A WHILE, with a deep sigh, she said she had been there a long time and that it would soon be dawn. She sat on the side of the bed and put on her nightgown. After carefully pulling it down over her hips and smoothing it over her breasts, she sat up erectly and brushed back her hair with both hands.

"Now, Steve," she said in a firm commanding manner as if reminding me that I had become obligated to tell her what she wanted to know, "you're going to tell me the truth. And only the honest-to-God truth. I've got to know. Did Guthry make love to that girl down on the island? Did he? One way or the other—it doesn't matter about that—but did they? That's what I've got to know."

I tried to convince her that I was being truthful and did not know anything about it and had not even seen them alone together. However, I had not forgotten his saying that he had seen Bonnie wading in the river and it was truthful to say I knew nothing about what had happened at that time.

"Do you swear that's the truth, Steve? Don't lie to me about this. Please don't. It's so important to me. That's why I've got to know the truth. And that's why I came here—like this. You must know that now."

I told her I would swear it was the truth.

"Well, I don't know what to think now." She paused, taking a deep breath, and closed her eyes as she slowly shook her head for several moments. "Guthry was so evasive about it—he would hardly say anything. That's what made me so suspicious—every thought about it was torture. And I'm still not sure in my own mind. If everybody else down there made love to her, why didn't he? It's not like him to stay away from a halfway pretty girl when she's available. I know him so well. He hasn't changed that much since he stopped traveling on the road. But maybe this time he did stay away. It's possible. I'm going to keep after him, though. I've got to be completely convinced one way or the other. It's such agony not to be sure—to be so uncertain—not to know what to believe. That's why I couldn't go to sleep tonight—I had to come in here—like this—and do anything to find out about Guthry and her."

She leaned close to me.

"This is going to be a secret, Steve. In here tonight. Every minute of it. You'll keep the secret, won't you, Steve? Not a word about it ever to be said—no matter what. Will you promise me?"

As soon as I promised her, she kissed me lightly on the forehead and squeezed my hand.

"Thank you, Steve. I know I can trust you."

Releasing my hand, she put both arms around my neck and held me close to her. Her body trembled as if she had been shaking with cold shivers.

"Don't hate me," she pleaded. "Please don't hate me. I couldn't help it. God knows I couldn't help it!"

A moment after that she got up and crossed the room. And after the faint click of the lock, I could barely hear the sound of the door of my room being

opened and closed, and then there was silence through-
out the house.

The dim moonlight had vanished by that time, probably because of the clouding of the sky, and it was in
the dark of night as I lay there with eyes wide open
for a long time thinking about what had happened and
wondering what Guthry would do if he found out about
it.

I admired Guthry and was glad to have an uncle like
him and I had been so pleased when he invited me to
come to Unionville for the summer and then took me
on my first fishing trip on the river. Thinking about all
that made me feel guilty about what I had done, as if
I had lied to him or stolen something from him, although I had no feeling of being sorry it had happened,
and I tried to convince myself that nothing would have
taken place if Aunt Rosemary had not wanted it that
way.

I had never seen Aunt Rosemary before coming to
Unionville for the summer. And since I was related to
her only because she was married to Guthry, I told myself that no real kinship existed even though I did call
her Aunt Rosemary. Finally, all tension and worry going at the first light of dawn, I had closed my eyes and
then had slept until the middle of the morning.

When I had finished dressing, I opened the door and
went to the hall. The door of Guthry and Aunt Rosemary's room was open and I could see that the double-
bed had been made smooth and tidy and the curtains
had been closed over the windows to keep out the daytime glare and heat of the summer sun. Aunt Rose-

mary's dressing table had an orderly row of small per-
fume bottles and powder boxes and her hand-mirror
and several combs and hairbrushes had been arranged
in precise positions. Stuck into the frame of the large
mirror on the wall above the dressing table were several photographs of Guthry and his sample cases at a
railroad depot and one picture of him standing in front
of a drummers' hotel.

I still had heard no sounds in the house and I was
sure Aunt Rosemary had gone downtown. As soon as I
got to the kitchen, though, I saw that she was sitting
at the table and reading the newspaper.

"Good morning, Steve," she said, looking up and
speaking in an even tone of voice without a trace of a
smile or a frown.

"Good morning, Aunt Rosemary," I said weakly, all at
once feeling a nervous twitching in my arms and
shoulders.

She got up and went to the stove.

"Sit down at the table, Steve. I've kept your breakfast
warm for you."

By turning my head slightly, I could see her at the
stove, and as long as she faced that direction I could not
keep from looking at her. She was wearing a tight-
fitting, light-brown, cotton dress but, with the vivid
memory of the night, she might as well have been completely naked, because what I saw was the shapely rise
of her legs and the soft contour of her hips and the fullness of her rounded breasts. And I knew the softness of
her hands and the warm clinging sensations of her kisses.

I was still staring at her when she suddenly turned

174

as if she had felt my sighting of her. After that momen-
tary glance she brought the breakfast plate to me. I began eating hurriedly and did not look up when she sat
down at the other end of the table. She did not pick
up the newspaper to continue reading and it seemed as
if several minutes had passed before anything was said.

"I've been thinking, Steve," I heard her say slowly in
the same even tone of voice. "It's something very important."

She had paused then, and I looked at her across the
table.

"Steve, I'm going to ask you to forget everything that
happened—last night—everything. It's not only to be a
secret—I want you to put it out of your mind and keep
it out. Don't even let yourself think it was something
you dreamed. Nothing happened. You understand? I
was so wrought up—so distressed and worried. I was
desperate—I love Guthry very much—and to think that
another woman—I couldn't sleep with him when I
wasn't sure—and I had to do something to hurt him—
if he had been unfaithful. And I wanted to find out the
truth somehow—I was too upset to believe he was telling
me the truth. But you told me the truth about him,
didn't you, Steve? You didn't lie, did you, Steve? You
didn't see him go off with that girl—make love to her—"

Putting her hands over her face, she began crying and
sobbing helplessly. Soon she leaned over the table,
burying her face in her arms, and sobbed so violently
that her whole body was trembling. I sat there not
knowing what to do. And then presently she asked me
to get a towel so she could dry her tears.

When I came back with the towel, Aunt Rosemary had almost stopped crying and was no longer leaning over the table. Taking the towel, she pressed it against her eyes and wiped the tears from her cheeks. After brushing back her hair the way she did with both hands, she got up and opened the door to the kitchen porch. She stood there in the bright sunlight of the morning for several moments as if thinking about something she was going to say.

When I stood up, she glanced at me for an instant as though still uncertain about what she would say to me. Suddenly she turned completely around so I could not see her face.

"Steve, your uncle said he wanted you to go down to the store as soon as you finished eating breakfast," she told me then in a firm voice, still not looking at me. "He wants you to help him with several things to be done. There are some large crates of new stock to be unpacked and sorted, for one thing. It needs to be done right away. He told me to let you sleep and not wake you up this morning. But it's already very late and he's expecting you. You'd better go now."

She moved several steps backward from the door and stood far away when I started to leave. She stayed there until I had left the house and gone down the porch steps.

"Wait a minute, Steve," I heard her say. "There's something I want to tell you. I mean, about something else. I forgot all about it till just now. I meant to tell you sooner."

I stopped at once, turning around and looking at her in the doorway, and wondered if that could be her way of letting me know she wanted me to stay there instead of going downtown to help Guthry.

"Steve, I told you that I was going to arrange some dates for you with some of the nicest girls in town, didn't I? You remember, don't you? Well, I haven't forgotten, either. But I've decided not to do anything about it. It wouldn't be wise, would it? No. Of course not. It wouldn't be a wise thing to do. It's different now that you've come back from that fishing trip to Summertime Island. One of those girls might get into trouble. You know what I mean—you might get her into trouble. That's why I think you'd better go looking around yourself—and find somebody like—what's-her-name—Bonnie. That's it—Bonnie. There are girls like her in town—so I've heard."

She smiled for the first time that morning.

"Anyway, you'll find somebody like her," she said with a slight tilting of her head as she went back into the house, "or somebody like me."

I did not know what to do then. I knew I should hurry down to the hardware store to help Guthry, but that was not what I wanted to do then. Aunt Rosemary must have known what I was thinking, because she closed the door with a loud slam. Whether she actually locked the door or not, I thought I heard the clicking of the lock to keep me from getting back into the house.

I waited on the path near the back porch, hoping to see her at the kitchen window, but she stayed out of sight. After a while I went to the front of the house, and even tried to see her at one of the other windows, but she was never within sight again anywhere.

3

THE DISTANCE WAS SHORT, but it seemed like the longest walk I had ever taken by the time I had gone down Glenwood Street and went through the courthouse square and got to the hardware store. Every step of the way, no matter how fast I walked and how determined I was, had been unwilling and painful. Even though I had stopped several times, wanting to turn around and go back, I had made myself keep on going until I walked into Guthry's store. Then it was too late to go back to the house.

By the time I had reached the store, I was worried and nervous and ashamed to look Guthry straight in the face. I knew I could never tell him about Aunt Rosemary being in my room during the night, and certainly nothing about what had happened, and that that was being deceitful. Besides, I had promised her never to say a word about it to anybody. I was so distressed by then that I wished I could go away somewhere as soon as possible so I would not have to face Guthry everyday during the rest of the summer.

There were several men in the store that morning and I recognized right away the familiar sound of Troy Pickett's loud voice.

"Hell, I was just only going about my business like I always do when I've got a load of freight and express to deliver," Troy was saying. "That's my ordinary habit. My brother done the best he could while I was down there fishing on the river, but he got behind and I was just trying to catch up and hurry and get everything delivered to the stores this morning early. Storekeepers want their merchandise on hand right at the start for Saturday business. That's natural. Saturday's when the country people come to town to spend what money they've got. Everybody knows that. That's why I was in such a big hurry this morning. I was trying to help out the storekeepers."

I could see Guthry looking down at the floor with a slow shaking of his head. If he had seen me come into the store, he was too absorbed in thought to speak to me.

"You wouldn't done a thing like that for just pure meanness, now would you, Troy?" one of the men in the crowd asked him.

Guthry glanced directly at me then but said nothing.

"Meanness ain't the name for it—there's a better reason than that," Troy said. "Hell, I've been making blacks jump all my life. They don't appreciate it, but I keep on doing it for their own good. You can't call that meanness. It's a big help to them to learn they'd better jump when they see a white man coming—like you learn a dog to keep his muddy paws off you by kicking him in the belly a few times. What the hell! It keeps the smart niggers from getting knocked down and hurt. That keeps them in their place—learning to jump or die. Niggers don't need no schoolbooks to learn a simple little thing like that."

"What happened to him then, Troy? Did he jump quick enough not to die?"

"Goddam if I know. That's his worry—not mine. But I know this much. If he don't die, it ought to learn him to keep out of my way from now on. When I see a black out there in the street taking his time about getting out of my way, you don't see me wearing out the brakes on my truck slowing down for him. That's what happened to that nigger this morning—he didn't have the sense to jump when I came down the street."

"Won't the police chief be after you, Troy?" somebody asked him.

"Naw. He tried that once but couldn't never get nobody to testify against me."

"What's the name of that colored, Troy?"

"Duke Hopkins. He's that stuck-up mulatto half-white half-black bastard who teaches at the nigger school and runs a little barbershop over on Prospect Avenue in their part of town. He's been around here for the past year or so. He came down here from somewhere up in Kentucky. That makes him think he's better than niggers born down here in Tennessee and can act different. But I learned him."

"Troy, ain't he the one you took fishing with you this past week down on Summertime Island?"

"I'm a sonofabitch!" said Troy, speaking out in his loud voice. "Guthry Henderson took him along—not me. He's Guthry's nigger. I don't own up to knowing nothing about him and don't never want to."

After Troy and the other men had left the store, Guthry told me about Duke having been knocked down and run over by Troy's truck earlier that morning. A man who had witnessed the hit-and-run said that Troy evidently had speeded up his truck when he saw Duke crossing Prospect Avenue and at first everybody there thought Duke had been killed and that it was useless to take him to the hospital.

"I phoned the hospital," Guthry said, "and they told me he's pretty badly banged-up with both legs broken, and some of his ribs, too, but the doctor said he's going to be all right other than that. It's lucky his skull didn't get cracked wide open—the way Troy was aiming at him.

"It'll take money that Duke doesn't have to stay in the hospital as long as he'll have to and I'm going around town and take up a collection to help him out. I won't have too much trouble raising some money for him—except I won't get a dime from Troy Pickett. Troy was sure at first he'd killed Duke—he even boasted in here a while ago that he'd tried to run over him hard enough to kill him. You remember how Troy's been saying he was going to get even with Duke for wrestling him to the ground—and for not calling him Mister Troy on the island—and for other reasons—but I didn't think he'd go that far. But he's Troy Pickett—and he did."

I told Guthry I wanted to go right away to the hospital to see Duke.

"Go right ahead, Steve. He'll appreciate that. Everything here can wait. There's no big hurry now about the unpacking. Ask him if he wants some of his books to read and we'll get them to him. And tell Duke not to worry about the hospital bill because I'll see to it that it's taken care of somehow."

I started to leave, but I had to stop before I got to the street door. When I turned around, Guthry asked me if I had changed my mind about going to the hospital.

"I'm going to see Duke," I told him as quickly as I could. "But—Guthry—then I'm going home."

"Going home?" he repeated with a puzzled expression coming over his face. "You mean—back to Memphis?"

I nodded. "I want to—I've got to."

"Why?"

Facing him then, I knew I could never tell him the real reason for my leaving Unionville after only one week of the whole summer. I was not even able to look straight at him after a few moments and I had to turn my head aside.

"Why, Steve?" he insisted.

"Just because—I want to."

"You're homesick, Steve," he said in a kindly way after a brief moment.

"Guthry—I don't know about that—but—"

"I understand, Steve. And I'm not surprised. After all the excitement of going on the camp-out—well, there's not much for a boy your age to do in a small place like Unionville all summer. And you're a city boy, too. Go on back home to Memphis. That's the best thing."

He put his hand on my shoulder and shook me gently.

"But, Steve, maybe next summer you'll want to come

back and stay longer. We'll go down to Summertime Island again, too. But it won't be with Troy Pickett—I'll have my own truck by then. And maybe by that time the road will be improved—bridges over the creeks and the sink holes filled in. And maybe we can persuade your Aunt Rosemary to go with us the next time. She won't be like another Bonnie around the place day and night—but she's a fine cook and good company and that's a lot better for a man in the long run. I got mighty tired of eating my own cooking down there."

I had reached the street door when Guthry called to me.

"Steve, tell Duke about next summer and let him know we'll want him to go with us. I wouldn't want to go back to the island again without him. You wouldn't, either, would you, Steve?"

About the Author

From the day of his birth in Coweta County, Georgia, until he reached the age of twenty, Erskine Caldwell rarely lived longer than a year in one place. The son of a Presbyterian minister, he left home at fourteen to wander through the Deep South, Mexico, and Central America. When he was seventeen, he enrolled at Erskine College, Due West, S.C., but remained only a short time. His next attempt to complete his education was when he entered the University of Virginia on a scholarship, and there he began writing short stories. Later he attended the University of Pennsylvania, and then spent eight years in Maine, where he wrote *Tobacco Road* and *God's Little Acre*. The latter, which the *Saturday Review* called "one of the finest studies of Southern poor whites that has ever come into our literature," is probably the most widely read contemporary American novel. During these years, he worked as a seaman, cotton picker, cabdriver, bodyguard, cub reporter, cook, and waiter.

Best known for his novels and short stories, Mr. Caldwell is also a journalist of note, having been a newspaper and radio correspondent in Europe during World War II. Once married to the *Life* photographer Margaret Bourke-White, Mr. Caldwell now lives in Florida with his present wife, Virginia. They spend a good deal of time traveling, both in the United States and abroad. His most recent books include *The Last Night of Summer, Close to Home,* and *Miss Mamma Aimee.*